DARKNESS WITHIN

DARKNESS AHEAD OF US #1

LEIF SPENCER

First published in Great Britain in 2020.

No part of this publication may be reproduced, stored in a retrieval system, or transmitted, in any form or by any means, without the express written permission of the publisher except for the use of brief quotations in a book review.

All characters and events in this publication are fictitious and any resemblance to real persons, living or dead, is purely coincidental.

All rights reserved.

Darkness Within © 2020 Leif Spencer
www.lspencerauthor.com

Cover by Holly Jameson
www.hollyjameson.co.uk

For Susan, who is the ideal quarantine partner.

ALSO BY LEIF SPENCER

THE END WE SAW (Novella Series)
Stolen Visions

Chased by Guilt

Misplaced Mercy

Forlorn Redemption

All We Have Left

THE END WE SAW (Omnibus)
The End We Saw (The Complete Series)

EXCLUSIVE FOR NEWSLETTER SUBSCRIBERS
After the Pulse (Short Story)

DARKNESS AHEAD OF US
Darkness Within

ACKNOWLEDGMENTS

Lauren, you're more important than you'll ever know.

Thank you, Gemma, for this household is now addicted to Animal Crossing. Next time, please order just the one copy (and keep it).

Thank you, Isabel, for picking up all remaining plot holes, typos and errors and for listening to me ramble on about all the unimportant stuff floating around my head. (Look! No Oxford comma!)

Thank you, Susan, for doing the boring job you do.

Thank you, Elizabeth from Women of the Apocalypse over on Facebook, for naming Oreo. It's a fantastic name!

And without Esther, half of my stories wouldn't have a title. Thank you.

Thank you, Stephanie and Misty, for reading and being so supportive.

I would like to thank the people who are delivering my shopping, and the people who are delivering my pizza during Covid-19. You're making it possible for me to stay inside and I'm grateful.

I would like to thank the people who are posting art, comics and stories for brightening my days.

I would like to thank the people who are posting recipes for sending me on a baking spree. Enough with the banana bread.

And, of course, I would like to thank every reader for supporting us authors by buying our books.

Lastly, I would like to thank some more people who have made it possible for me to write my stories: Dave (who's taught me about guns), John (who always offers invaluable feedback), Colin (who's created more than one butterfly effect in my world), Bryan (who sounds strangely awake after midnight), and Anthony (whose stories I can't wait to read).

1

IT HAPPENED ON A MILD DAY AT THE END OF JUNE, AND JUST like most people, Anna Greene wasn't prepared.

She was lying on the sofa mindlessly browsing Netflix with her dog Oreo curled up against her legs when the world went dark.

It was close to midnight and up until that point, it had been a normal day.

Cold, unsweetened oats for breakfast (she was trying to lose weight *yet again*), a homemade protein bar for lunch. She'd missed a phone call from her father during her lunch break and had yet to listen to his—she assumed angry, he was always angry—voicemail, but customers had been particularly entitled and irritating at work, and she'd left her personal phone in her locker.

Every now and then, she just needed a lunch break where she did nothing but sit on a bench and stare into her empty Tupperware.

After work, a casual date she'd met on one of her many apps had stood her up. Sitting alone at the small table for two in the middle of a pizzeria, she'd ended up ordering herself a large pizza and felt judged by every other guest as she ate, no matter whether they'd even noticed her or not.

Yes. It had been a perfectly normal day for Anna Greene.

A burst of static filled the living room with a loud hiss. The dim light from the lamp next to the radiator flickered and died at the same time as the television. Above her head, the fan slowed, then stopped spinning altogether.

An eerie quiet settled over her flat and for a moment, Anna thought she'd gone deaf.

Oreo placed his head on her thigh and whined, his ears back, the whites of his eyes showing.

Anna frowned, grabbed her phone and tapped the screen. "What the…" She glared at her faint reflection on the dead screen, her double chin making her appear at least ten years older than she was. She pressed down on the power button, waiting for the phone to reboot.

Why was it so quiet?

Tilting her head, Anna listened for the low hum of traffic coming from the main road.

Nothing.

Unease crept up her neck, prickled her skin.

"It's just a power cut," Anna muttered, unsure if her meagre attempt at comforting words was aimed at herself or the dog. She reached for her Kindle and opened the case.

It didn't turn on either.

At the age of thirty-seven, Anna still didn't know how to check her fuse box—didn't even know where to find it—but she reckoned opening the window might answer a few of her questions.

Outside, the moon shone impossibly bright, a thick silver disc hanging above the horizon seemingly just out of reach. Two cars appeared to have broken down in the middle of the road, both drivers fumbling with their bonnets.

Anna looked up. The sky was a black canvas sprinkled with gleaming dots.

She leaned forward, stretching in search of the traffic lights further down the road. Her gaze drifted along the pavement. Every single streetlight was out. As were the traffic lights.

Harlow, a town on the border of London and Hertfordshire, had been plunged into darkness.

It was as though the world had stopped, and Anna heard crickets chirping in the park across the road.

"Guess there's no need to find the fuse box," Anna said to Oreo.

The silence didn't last long. Around her, windows opened and doors slammed. People trickled into the street wearing dressing gowns and slippers, some shouting, others laughing.

Anna shut the window and turned to her dog. "Oh no." She walked over to where her laptop sat on the dining table. She closed her eyes and pressed the power button, hoping the laptop wasn't just as dead as her phone. Opening one eye, she let out a sigh as the laptop turned on and displayed the Lenovo logo.

"Thank—" She froze as the screen turned blue and an error code appeared at the top. Anna didn't know what the numbers meant and instinctively reached for her phone to google the code, momentarily forgetting that her phone, too, was dead.

"You watched me charge this before we went out for our walk, right?" she asked Oreo, and he whined again, his rear pressed against the edge of his bed. A string of saliva hung from his snout.

Was he picking up on her unease? She'd heard of pets sensing earthquakes hours before they happened and eyed him with a frown.

Oreo was a small black and white Border Collie and a bit

of a wuss. His bark might scare off potential intruders but if they persisted, they'd soon discover that he was all bark and no bite.

On the table, the laptop screen flickered and died.

Anna scowled. Power cuts didn't kill laptops and cars.

It had to be a coincidence.

But what if this was something worse than a power cut? Something that couldn't be fixed in a couple of hours.

At this point in time, she owned two litres of bottled water (didn't the government recommend twenty or so?) and only because Sarah had brought them over several months ago—Anna couldn't even remember what they'd been for. Since she only drank tap water, the bottles had been gathering dust and dog hair in a corner of her kitchen.

Her pantry, if it could be called that—it was more of a cupboard—consisted of roughly a week's worth of tinned chickpeas and chopped tomatoes. The remaining spaghetti in the pasta jar on top of her kitchen counter would make one more meal at most.

She had three rolls of toilet paper left.

Supermarkets delivered daily if you were willing to pay; why bother stocking up?

Anna stood in her kitchen and stared at her fridge.

If the power didn't come back on in the next twenty-four hours, she'd lose the chicken thighs and the cheese pizza unless she cooked them before they spoilt—but how? Without power, neither her oven nor her stove would work.

The thought of eating raw chicken made her shudder. Her sister would probably pickle it or whatever it was you did to preserve raw meat.

Anna owned no bathtub, so she couldn't fill it with water, and while she stood in her kitchen staring at her fridge, she realised not only was she not prepared, she didn't know anybody who was.

She didn't have an emergency bag ready stuffed under her bed, didn't own a secluded cabin in the woods and had no acquaintances serving in the army.

She *knew* about these things because of the books she'd read, but it had never occurred to her to actually prepare.

Anna considered herself an introvert with few friends, but she talked to her sister at least once a week. Sarah and Anna had discussed emergencies once. It had been more of a joke, one evening after a few glasses of red wine, and not an actual attempt at serious preparation. But if they ever found themselves in such a situation, Sarah would drive to Harlow because Anna's flat was easier to defend. Located on the top floor, intruders could only come from one direction, and Oreo would alert them of anyone entering the building.

"If the phones stop working, you stay put," Sarah had said giggling into her glass, but they hadn't considered a situation where phones, cars and trains didn't work.

Sarah lived about forty miles away and Anna briefly considered hiking along the A120, but it would take her three, if not four days, and by the time she'd knock on Sarah's door, Sarah might be knocking on Anna's.

"And for years they wandered through England, never finding each other," Anna said dramatically to her fridge door. "Until that one fateful day, five years later, when they'd both reach the same settlement, so haggard and pale they would fail to recognise each other."

Anna blinked and turned to Oreo. "What am I saying? It's just a power cut." Oreo whined in reply, but before Anna could say anything else, movement outside caught her attention. Looking out of her kitchen window, she watched a couple of teenagers run through the streets, shouting at each other.

One threw eggs at a house, another a brick into a car's windscreen.

Should she call the poli—

She couldn't.

She couldn't call anyone.

Her heart pounded in her chest and she knelt, waiting for Oreo to settle in front of her. He nuzzled her neck, his nose cold and wet.

She needed to stay calm.

Consider the facts.

A simple power cut wouldn't affect her phone, Kindle and laptop.

Then there were the two broken-down cars.

She glanced at the clock on the wall. The hands had stopped moving at five to twelve.

"This isn't just a power cut," she whispered, and Oreo whined, offering his paw as if trying to figure out what Anna wanted from him.

An idea struck her. "Be right back." Anna grabbed her car keys from the shoe rack next to the front door and slipped into her flip flops. She ran downstairs, exiting the building through the back and found her car. She pressed the button to unlock it.

Nothing happened.

Opening the door manually, she gripped the steering wheel with a trembling hand and sat down. She slid the key into the ignition.

Turned it.

Nothing.

Her gut tightened.

Her phone, laptop, Kindle and now her car.

No. Anna wasn't prepared for any kind of emergency whatsoever, but she knew from the books she read how fast savage instincts replaced civilised manners, even if she'd never really believed it. The books had also taught her that inaction or sticking to well-known, yet pointless routines was what killed most people during disasters. They died trying to retrieve their overhead luggage after an emergency landing or running back into their burning houses to fetch their keys.

Of course, some died out of sheer stupidity. Trying to take a picture of a tsunami rushing at them or posing for a selfie next to a burning plane.

Survivors either had luck on their side, or they acted quickly—instead of freezing they ran for cover or, if stuck inside, found an exit.

Everyone else remained paralysed by the adrenaline surge and the resulting brain fog, making all the wrong decisions if they were even able to react at all.

Anna had two options. She could either assume it was a power cut and settle back down on the sofa, cuddle Oreo for a bit before going to sleep or she could conclude that a city-wide power outage, two broken-down cars, a dead phone and a laptop displaying a blue screen were too much of a coincidence.

And, of course, her own car.

Frankly, she preferred option one.

What was the worst that could happen if she went to sleep?

Anna locked her car and shuffled back inside. She tried to recall the causes of these disasters in her books. If a solar flare, an EMP or perhaps a major cyber-attack had caused this, the world was in a lot of trouble.

Supermarkets would be emptied with no one to restock them. Fresh food would perish within a week or two, and once the tinned goods were gone, people would starve.

Tinned food and medicine would soon be worth more than gold.

If the broken-down cars, the streetlights, her laptop and her phone were just a coincidence, Anna would laugh at herself come morning and have a funny story to tell her sister right after asking her what the bottled water gathering dust in her kitchen had been for.

Anna opened her cupboard and stared at her chickpeas, scratching the nape of her neck.

All her money was safe in the bank. She laughed dryly. So safe that she'd never see it again. Cards were accepted everywhere these days. Did anyone still carry cash?

Not that cash would remain useful for much longer, but it wouldn't hurt to have some during those first few days when most people likely still thought the world would go back to normal.

She closed the cupboard and turned to her dog. "Tell me I'm being silly, and this is just my overactive imagination." Oreo had retreated into his bed, too busy licking his privates to even acknowledge she'd said something.

What else would she need if this truly was an attack on the national grid?

Her gaze swept the kitchen as she mentally ticked off items on a checklist.

Thankfully, she didn't need any medicine on prescription. She'd definitely run out if that were the case. The one time she'd needed them, she'd regularly left it to the last day to get her prescription refilled.

More than once she'd had to beg her GP's receptionist to please make an exception and bother the doctor after hours so Anna could nip into the pharmacy next door before it closed for the day. Come to think of it, there was probably a note in her file: please don't prescribe anything to this patient if it can be avoided.

She found an open packet of ibuprofen, expired antibiotics from when she'd had her tooth abscess and some paracetamol on a shelf next to her crockery, but that was the extent of her medical supplies.

Her gaze drifted to the knife block, and she pulled out a

carving knife. Knives were the only weapons in her flat. The characters in her books had rifles, guns and baseball bats. Anna didn't even know *how* to fire a gun—she barely knew the difference between a pistol and a hunting rifle. There was a thing called a trigger, and she'd heard of a hammer.

And of course, you needed ammunition.

Oreo was her only defence. She'd tried ballet as a child and had attended Kung-Fu classes during her university years, but her right knee was bust, and one swift kick would be the end of any fight.

"Ballet isn't very helpful now, is it, Mum?" Anna rolled her eyes walking past the urn containing her mother's ashes. She stopped in the doorway to the living room and narrowed her eyes. She played the violin. Not helpful either.

Although, she thought with a shrug, the instrument could be used as firewood. With a little help from her book collection, she might be able to cook those chicken thighs over an open fire in the communal patch of grass the letting agency called a garden.

As Anna opened the door to her bedroom, she noticed her running shoes in the hallway by the front door. She ran two to three miles several times a week to strengthen her knee—a skill that could have possibly helped her outrun a zombie, at least for twenty minutes or so, but unfortunately this didn't seem to be a zombie apocalypse.

However, it occurred to her that if the power wasn't coming back, she'd definitely shed the few pounds that she'd been trying to lose for what felt like the better part of the last decade, and this time she wouldn't be able to bin the diet *just for the night* and order herself a curry.

That's *if* she survived long enough for the weight to fall off.

If an EMP or a solar flare had caused the power cut, most people wouldn't last that long. The people who survived catastrophes of this magnitude usually possessed at least one valuable skill.

Anna didn't think of herself as someone knowledgeable or smart. She worked in a call centre, listening to customers complain all day long. But if she was right and phones were a thing of the past, then all that job had taught her was how to deal with angry people.

Then again, perhaps that was useful after all, just like living on the top floor.

"What do *you* do in emergencies?" she asked Oreo as she stepped over his bed, but the dog had gone to sleep, stretching all four paws into the air. "No earthquakes, eh?"

The BBC and the government would attempt to use the radio to communicate with the nation, but Anna hadn't owned a radio since she was a teenager.

Without the internet, she had no way of finding out what was happening outside.

All she'd ever know was that on a mild day at the end of June, Harlow had gone dark.

And most people had gone to bed thinking it was just a power cut.

Something that'd be fixed by the time they woke up.

It gave her a single night to prepare.

Teenagers might use this night to throw bricks and eggs at cars and windows, but they wouldn't understand the seriousness of the situation. Only that the police hadn't turned up.

The Tesco on Edinburgh Way was open twenty-four hours and if she filled a wheeled suitcase and as many of those giant blue IKEA bags as she could carry with supplies, she might just survive for a few weeks. The cash registers wouldn't work, of course, and it would be pitch-black inside, but if she hurried, she might be able to sneak in through one of the exits at the back while the staff were busy trying to figure out what to do.

She needed to dig through her camping equipment in the loft, find her torch, and then she'd be ready to stock up on medicine, water, tinned food, multivitamins, pasta, dog food, candles and toilet paper.

And, if possible, a small analogue radio and batteries. She didn't know if it would work, but it was worth a try.

And once back home, she'd lock the door and wait it out.

Or laugh at herself come morning.

Anna hoped for the latter.

2

CHRISTINE HUGHES HATED WORKING ON THE TILL AT TESCO at night. The squeaky chair was uncomfortable, and her back was already sore from her day shift at the hospital.

While stacking shelves was far worse for her poor back, it was at least peaceful, unlike the checkout where she had to deal with rowdy drunks making lewd comments about her uniform and fend off odd, lonely people who just wanted to chat.

Chris didn't want to chat, especially not at 11pm—she wasn't paid nearly enough for that. She just wanted to make enough money to feed her family and pay the bills.

Why did teenagers have to eat so much? And what was going on with their bodies growing like weeds? Tom was a good kid, but lately it seemed as though he needed new clothes every other month. And not just shirts and jeans. Every time he went up a size, he also needed a new set of clothes for both school and football.

Her husband was a kind man, but he'd been struggling with crippling depression for a few years, and it didn't look as if he was going to win the fight any time soon. Lester had lost his job after a series of terrible performance reviews almost two months ago, and at first Chris had been upset with him. She'd tried not to show it, of course—she didn't want to be quite that cruel.

Especially since he'd taken the battle against his invisible enemy seriously from the start. He diligently attended his therapy sessions, took his tablets like clockwork, and Chris knew it wasn't his fault his serotonin levels were unstable. But as a nurse, she wasn't making anywhere near enough to support a family, and now she was juggling shifts at Tesco on top of the ones at Princess Alexandra Hospital.

She couldn't remember when she'd last slept for more than three hours at a time and had stopped looking in the mirror when getting ready for work. She didn't need to see her sunken eyes and the dark circles under them to know she looked like a teenager going through a goth phase—only with grey strands peppering her hair and crow's feet crinkling her eyes.

At least they only had the one son. They'd wanted more, but giving birth to Tom had almost killed her, and she'd decided right there and then, that it wouldn't happen again and had her tubes tied.

The stench of alcohol wafted through the air, and Chris held her breath. A man with a scraggly beard staggered towards her, his loosely tied bathrobe revealing naked legs. She prayed that he was wearing underwear as he placed a bottle of vodka onto the conveyor belt.

Crumbs dotted his beard, his small, red-rimmed eyes unfocused and glassy. He reached for his wallet, then promptly dropped it. Bending down to retrieve it, he lost his balance and tumbled to the dirty floor where he sat, giggling to himself.

Chris pressed the button that alerted her manager before leaning over the belt to make sure the man on the floor was all right. The odds of Mike actually showing his bloated face were slim to none, but she wasn't going to deal with a drunk by herself in the middle of the night.

She pressed the button again and considered waving over the security guard who was busy studying the magazines by the entrance.

Lately, Mike had spent his shifts flirting with Chris' colleague, Lily, somewhere in the back instead of doing his job of managing the store.

Chris waited, sighed and rubbed her eyes before turning her attention back to the man on the floor. "Are you—"

The overhead lights flickered, and a high-pitched hissing sound filled the air. Her eardrums vibrated. It was as if a swarm of bees had found its way inside the supermarket, and Chris covered her ears with her hands.

The lights died. One after another like falling dominoes, plunging the shop into darkness.

"Great," Chris muttered. "Just great." A power cut at this hour meant that she'd be sent home early and probably wouldn't get paid for her entire shift. She glanced at her smartwatch, silently calculating her pay for the night so far, but the clock face didn't light up. She waved her hand—sometimes the watch didn't pick up on the fact that she'd lifted her arm—but the screen remained dark.

She tapped it.

Pressed the button to activate the menu.

Nothing.

Dim moonlight came in through the front windows.

"Hey, who turned the lights off?" the man on the floor asked, his features indistinct in the dark, but Chris could hear the fear in his voice.

From her experience with drunk people at the hospital, she knew how quickly fear could turn into anger.

She fumbled for her phone and tapped the screen.

It didn't turn on either. It was only six months old, and

she distinctly remembered charging it at the hospital only two hours ago.

What was going on?

She pressed the button to alert her manager again but remembered it wouldn't do anything during a power cut. Chris stood and scowled. She didn't want to leave the till while the drunk man was nearby, but she had to find Mike.

The few customers who had been roaming the aisles had abandoned their shopping trolleys and were trying to find the exit. Chris couldn't see them—the moonlight didn't reach the back of the shop—but she heard shuffling steps, people bumping into trolleys and shelves, and the security guard who'd stood by the door swearing at his walkie-talkie.

Something grabbed her ankle and a hand wrapped itself tightly around her leg. Chris shrieked, kicking with her other foot.

Still standing near the entrance, the security guard seemed to have remembered that he carried a torch. She heard him tap it a few times until a faint light flashed in streaks through the supermarket.

At her feet, the drunk man groaned, but his grip on her tightened. "Vodka?" He drew out the word like a toddler asking his mother for ice cream.

"Let me go," Chris shouted, and when he didn't, she kicked again, this time ramming her heel into his nose. The sickening crunch made her wince, but the kick had the desired effect. He let go, his hands clutching his face instead, and she ran before he could grab her again.

"Who's manning the till?" Mike asked when she pushed the doors to the back open and was hit square in the face by the brunt of his torch light. She squinted, shielding her eyes with one hand.

"Do you mind?" She pushed on his hand to angle the

torch towards the floor. "I had a drunk grab me. The button didn't work."

Mike huffed. "We're in the middle of a power cut in case you hadn't noticed."

"Are you sure it's just a power cut?" Chris frowned and pulled out her phone. "Both my phone *and* my watch have died."

"Well, you can't charge them right now, can you?" A patronising smile appeared on his lips, his tone gently mocking as if talking to a child. Chris scowled. He appeared taller than usual, standing with his back straight, puffing out his chest as though he thought this was his moment. His time to shine.

"No, I mean—" Chris shook her head. "Never mind." It wasn't her problem if Mike didn't want to listen.

He shoved a torch into her hand. "Take this and go back to the till. Wait there until you receive further instructions. The electrician will be here soon."

Chris was about to tell him that she had no intention of staying, but something made her nod instead. She wasn't paid enough to stick around and wait for people who, mere hours before, would have claimed to have been decent and law-abiding citizens, to ransack the supermarket. It would be easy for people to rush in and grab a few things with only Roland by the door.

And they would.

Especially in this part of town.

No. She was going home. To her family.

Mike grinned, probably happy to see her willing to obey his instructions like a good employee without objection, and she left him standing there without correcting him.

Chris grabbed her bag and car keys and snuck out through the back exit. She promptly collided with a young woman who was carrying several giant, blue IKEA bags and pulling a wheeled suitcase.

"I'm sorry," the woman mumbled, rolling the suitcase over Chris' foot in her attempt to reach the door before it closed. "I'm sorry."

"Excuse me?" Chris said. "This door is only for—"

The woman dropped her suitcase and brushed strands of short hair from her eyes. Chris lifted her torch. The woman seemed upset, her pupils shrinking away from the light. Chris frowned, taking in the woman's glistening, clammy skin. Behind her, only darkness loomed. All the streetlights were out. There was no light coming from inside any houses at all.

Darkness had crept in from all sides.

Chris blinked, goosebumps covering her arms.

"I'm trying to get supplies before everything is gone. Please?" Her voice was laced with the sort of despair Chris associated with homeless people begging at the shop entrance.

Chris tilted her head and pointed the torch at the ground, illuminating their feet. The woman wore pink trainers and hadn't bothered to tie her shoelaces. They were brown and crusted with dirt where they'd been dragged along the ground. "What do you mean *before everything is gone*?"

"This isn't just a power cut," the woman whispered, her left eye twitching as though she was sharing a secret.

Chris frowned, narrowing her eyes. Why did the weird ones always come out at night? And how did they always find *her*? Chris wondered, not for the first time, if she was some sort of magnet for the odd and lonely. In the dim light of the torch, Chris saw the woman had dark blonde hair and pale blue eyes. She didn't look like the usual suspects eager to spread conspiracy theories. Her hands weren't trembling, and her eyes were focused, albeit filled with fear.

Obviously nonplussed by Chris' frown, the woman took a step closer. "Your phone is dead, isn't it?"

Chris nodded, remembering her watch, and a wave of nausea rolled through her belly. She swallowed, tasting acid. What if this woman was right and this wasn't a power cut? Wasn't that what she'd *just* tried to tell Mike?

"Mine is dead as well. As are all the cars. I walked here from Fifth Avenue. Not a single one is working. This is far more than a simple power cut, and I'm not prepared. Are you prepared?" The woman's eyes flicked from Chris' face to her small bag and back to her face. "I just want to stock up on supplies before the rest of this town wakes up and realises something big has happened. Please?"

Chris traced her brow with a finger and considered the stranger's words. She always had enough food at home for at least a couple of weeks, but if this woman was right, she'd need more than food. "And then? What are you going to do once you have your supplies?"

"I'll go home and wait this out. Let everyone fight over what's left."

"But the government—"

"If this was—" the woman stopped, narrowing her eyes. "Believe me, I know how this must sound to you. But if this was an EMP or a cyber-attack, the government won't be able to do a thing. It'll take months to restore the power, and we'll all be starving by then."

"EMP?" Chris had heard the term before but didn't know what it meant.

"It's some form of magnetic pulse. It fries all electronics, and that's basically everything these days."

"Wouldn't the EU…wouldn't someone send help? Surely, they have plans for this sort of thing?"

"Maybe…if it's just Harlow or Essex…but what if it's not? Look, as far as I'm concerned, we have a choice. We can assume it's just a power cut, go home and go to sleep and listen to what the government has to say tomorrow. We can trust that they'll take care of us, and that we'll be receiving help. Or we can prepare for the worst and if it all falls apart, we'll have food. If it doesn't, we'll have a funny story to tell our friends."

Chris couldn't argue with the woman's logic. "And you're *sure* all of the cars have broken down?"

"Listen." The woman pressed her index finger against her lips. "Can you hear that?"

Chris squinted, then shook her head.

"Exactly. No traffic. Nothing. But if you don't believe me, why don't you go and check if your car starts? Mine didn't."

Chris shook her head. Odd or not, the woman appeared sober and coherent. Besides, being prepared wasn't the worst idea in the world. At least Lester would have something to laugh about if this turned out to be nothing more than a power cut after all.

"I believe you." Chris opened the door and gestured for the woman to follow her. "My name's Chris. What do you think we'll need? Just food?"

The smell of alcohol and rotten teeth assaulted her senses. Greasy hands wrapped themselves around her neck and squeezed. Chris tried to use the torch as a weapon, but the drunk man grabbed her wrist and the torch clattered to the floor.

"Where's my vodka?" he asked, as his fat fingers yanked her towards him.

Her vision swam, the edges darkening.

"I want my vodka."

3

"My name's An—" Before Anna could finish her sentence, the stench of alcohol invaded her nose and she froze. She knew this smell, knew it only too well from her childhood.

Thick fingers had gripped Chris' throat and were squeezing the life out of her. The small woman tried to hit her attacker with her torch, but he had already grabbed her slender wrist and she dropped the tool. A streak of light projected towards the ceiling as it clattered to the ground.

Anna watched, helpless, as the glass shattered, but before they were enveloped by darkness, she saw that the fingers belonged to a plump man wearing a fluffy bathrobe and pink bunny slippers. Oily brown hair stuck to his sweaty forehead, his nose and mouth smeared with fresh blood.

"Where's my vodka?"

The man's breath reeked of rotting gums. Fear paralysed her. Even the way he slurred his words sounded like her father when he was drunk. A flood of memories overwhelmed her, and she squeezed her eyes shut as though that could somehow stop them—even though it never did.

Her heart pounded as she watched her father's broad

frame approach with his hand raised and ready to—as he used to say—*smack some sense into her. You don't seem to have a lot of sense, Anna,* he'd say. *Hopefully, I can change that before it's too late.*

Anna instinctively brought both hands up to protect her head from her father's blows when a gurgling sound brought her back to the present. Sucking in a deep breath, she pushed her fear back down.

This wasn't her father, and Chris needed her help.

Anna's hands shook as she reached out, fumbling for Chris and her attacker in the darkness. She found oily hair and pulled on it. The man groaned, and Anna heard a sharp intake of breath come from her left as he let go of Chris, immediately followed by an angry cry. Moments later, bones crunched, and the man doubled over in pain. Anna released the fistful of hair she was still clutching as he crumbled, hitting the floor with a loud thud.

She grabbed Chris by the elbow, dragging her suitcase with her other hand and pulled the dazed woman towards the entrance where a security guard stood, brandishing his torch as though it were a weapon.

Chris waved at him, and he gave her a friendly nod.

Anna stopped to catch her breath, her limbs tingling with adrenaline. "Are you all right?"

Chris nodded, rubbing her throat. "You?"

"I think so." Anna focused on her breathing, waiting for her heartbeat to slow and for the blood to stop pounding in her ears. She felt dizzy and swayed, but Chris extended both her arms and held Anna steady. Just like her mum used to after one of her father's *outbursts*. Somehow, Chris knew not to hug her, not to step into her personal space and to offer her hands instead.

"Are you sure you're okay?" the small woman asked.

Anna smiled. "I'm sure."

Tesco was empty now—all the other customers seemed to have been ushered outside. The security guard stood with his back to them, staring into the darkness outside. Clearly, he was not expecting trouble from within the shop.

Anna wondered if he'd try to stop them once he realised what they were doing. *Of course, he would. That's his job.* "Shouldn't you let security know about that guy trying to strangle you?"

Chris coughed, taking deep breaths. "The last thing we want is attention, right?" She ran her fingers along her throat as if checking her windpipe for damage. "Let someone else find him. Unless you're prepared to answer dozens of questions while my manager calls the police and insists we wait for them to arrive."

"But he can't call them."

"Exactly my point but believe me, he *will* try, and he *will* insist we wait."

Anna shrugged. "If you say so. I'm Anna by the way." She retrieved a piece of paper from her jeans pocket. "I've brought a list of things I need." Zipping open her suitcase, she pulled out two more IKEA bags. "You can use these. Do you happen to know if this Tesco sells small radios?"

Chris nodded. "I'll go get two."

"Thank you. Grab a couple of torches as well. The one I had at home is fried." She didn't know what it meant that most electronic devices seemed to have stopped working, yet both Chris and the security guard carried functioning torches. Perhaps the shape of the Tesco, or the material of the building had shielded them.

Anna wished she'd paid more attention during physics classes at school.

Chris gave her a thumbs-up and grabbed the two bags. "Anything else?"

"Whatever you can think of to stay alive."

The two women hurried in opposite directions, and Anna worked her way from one end of the supermarket to the other, dashing through the aisles as quickly as possible. She threw supplies into her suitcase with one hand and struck the items off her list with the other, using her mouth to hold her small pencil. The wood had splintered at the end where she'd chewed on it and it tasted of graphite.

The encounter with the drunk man had left a bitter taste in her mouth, but the tension was easing, and the fear had died down to a small fluttering in her belly. Just like every time she thought of *him,* small waves of nausea washed over her.

"What do you think you're doing?" a stern voice asked from behind her.

Anna flinched, dropping the handle of her suitcase. She turned to find a scrawny man with a round, bloated face standing at the end of the aisle. She spotted a nametag on his jacket but couldn't read it from a distance.

"Shopping?" she said innocently. She flashed him her most charming smile, despite knowing that she probably wouldn't get away with her answer. It was worth a try, though.

It was always worth a try with men.

"The tills are closed. You need to leave this shop."

Anna opened her mouth, then hesitated. How many weeks' worth of food did she have if she grabbed her suitcase and ran? Would it be enough?

In that moment, Chris came around the corner holding several multipacks of baked beans. "Have you seen—" Spotting the man, she came to an abrupt halt.

He narrowed his eyes. "Christine?"

"Mike."

This had to be the manager Chris had mentioned. The expression on his face shifted. With his torch directly aimed at her face, Anna couldn't make out whether his features were relaxed or angry, but she assumed it was the latter by the way he puffed out his chest.

With his slick hair and neat uniform, he looked like the kind of man who did his job according to the rules in his workers' manual every day, but especially on a day like this. Loyal to his employer, he knew no flexibility, no mercy.

Desperate to please. And even more desperate to feel important.

"Security," he yelled, and Anna would have bet money on him not knowing the security guard's name. "Please detain these two women. They were trying to rob us. Her suitcase is full of stolen food."

"We're not trying to rob you," Anna protested. "Ring it up and I'll pay for it." She pulled out her wallet even though she knew she'd brought no cash with her. Only her credit card.

"I know your type." He sneered. "You're trying to take advantage of the situation. You're not dumb. You know that our tills aren't working during a power cut." He jabbed his finger in the direction of the security guard. "Why aren't you calling the police?"

"I can't call the police. Not without a working phone." The security guard was a tall man with broad shoulders and sharp eyes. "The shop is empty. Let's just lock up early and let them go. I'm sure you have Christine's details. Deal with it tomorrow."

Anna was about to protest when Mike turned to Chris, bristling. "You are fired." Anger had coloured his cheeks a bright red.

"Fine. If that's how you want to handle things." Chris scowled, tilting her head and exposing the marks on her neck. "A drunkard threatened me tonight. When I called my manager, he failed to show up, and when I finally found him and told him, he sent me back to the till with nothing but a torch during a power cut. And a few minutes later that same drunkard tried to strangle me." She spoke slowly, enunciating every word. "You'll be hearing from my solicitor, Mike."

Anna glanced at the security guard who stood between them and the exit like an immovable boulder. Adrenaline pooled in her stomach. Leaning closer to Chris she whispered, "I need the food. Please." If she didn't bring home enough supplies to last a few months, it would have all been for nothing. She'd have to venture out again. This time likely into a mass of panicked people fighting over scraps.

Anna scowled as Mike took a step in their direction. She feared men like him. They were unpredictable when upset. She'd spoken to the likes of him thousands of times at work. The type who was always right and always knew everything better. The type who refused to read the instruction manual, then called customer support because they'd broken their new bathroom cabinet while assembling it. The type who was entitled to compensation, of course, because they were just that important.

He wouldn't listen to her, and he definitely wouldn't listen to Chris. Tomorrow, he'd probably tell his mother that he'd known from the start that something was wrong and how he'd single-handedly saved Tesco during a late-night robbery. And if his mother asked why he'd failed to bring home supplies, he'd tell her that he had a plan.

His type always had a plan.

The security guard, on the other hand, appeared to be a sensible man.

So, Anna turned to him. "Is your walkie-talkie still working?"

He shook his head.

"And you said your phone isn't working either?"

"It's dead. Must have forgotten to charge it before work."

"It's not just your phone." Anna pulled out her own

mobile and pressed the power button for a few seconds, the screen angled towards the guard. "Something fried our electronics. This isn't just a power cut. A power cut doesn't affect walkie-talkies and it doesn't affect phones." She gestured towards the exit, pointing in the direction of the road. "The cars stopped working, too. All of them. At once. They're dead in the road. Like bricks." She waited for the security guard to meet her eyes. "If I were you, I'd leave now and take home enough food to keep your family safe. Don't forget vitamins, matches, candles and bottled water."

He narrowed his eyes, turning his phone around in his large hands. He pressed a few buttons and scowled.

"What's the worst that could happen if you listened to us and let us go?" Chris asked, her voice soft.

The guard rubbed his neck. "I don't know." His eyes flicked from Chris to Anna and back to Chris. He moved his jaw as though chewing on her words.

"Tomorrow, you'll come back, and you'll pay for what you've taken. They won't fire you. Not if I tell them that you were the only person to help me when I was attacked." Chris grinned, her white teeth shining in the light of the torch. "And you'll have a funny story to tell your wife."

Of course they'd fire him, Anna thought, but if she was right, nobody was going to come back the next day anyway and it wouldn't matter.

A smile tugged at the corners of his mouth while Chris spoke. "And what about you?" he asked.

Chris shrugged. "They have my details. It's not like I can disappear and not pay. I work for them."

"They might be right, Mike," the guard said. "You should do the same. Stock up on supplies. Go home. Just in case."

Mike's face was the colour of a ripe tomato. "I told you to detain these two women until the police pick them up."

"I don't think the police are coming, Mike." The guard

shoved his phone back into the pocket of his trousers. "You can le—"

"No." Mike spat. "Detain them or I will."

When the guard didn't move, Mike pulled a taser from his jacket. Anna blinked as he took a step towards Chris.

Aren't tasers illegal? Just as that thought flashed through her mind, Anna realised the world had already changed.

And would possibly never be the same again.

She watched, dumbfounded, as fury contorted Mike's face. His eyes darkened, and he reached for Chris as though possessed by rage.

Just like that. The transformation was complete. From a perfectly well-behaved member of society to a man tasering a woman. Convinced that he was well within his rights to do so.

Anna's stomach dropped. *Do something*, she told herself.

Chris' eyes widened. The security guard moved swiftly, stepping between Mike and Chris, his back to the small woman, and grabbed Mike's wrist.

"Let go," the guard grunted, his grip tightening, but Mike held on and pushed against the guard's stomach.

A flurry of movement. A sharp intake of breath followed by a punch. The guard's fist connected with Mike's face. A sickening crunch. Blood spurted from Mike's nose and he staggered. Both hands flew to his face, and the taser clattered to the floor.

"You're not going to get away with this," Mike screeched. Thick blood ran through his fingers.

"Get whatever else you need and leave," the security guard said to Chris and Anna. "I'll deal with him."

Anna didn't move. Couldn't move. She blinked, stared. Chris pulled on her elbow. "Come on!"

The coppery smell of blood brought bile to her mouth.

"Anna?"

Dazed, she shook her head and finally realised she had to move. She grabbed her bags and suitcase and followed Chris.

Ten minutes later, they stepped out into the night at the back of the Tesco, and Anna swallowed a sob. Her entire body was trembling.

Beside her, Chris' nostrils flared. The acrid smell of smoke hung in the air.

"Something is burning," Anna said.

"Yes," Chris replied softly. "If you're right, a whole lot of things will be burning very soon."

"You don't happen to own one of those old cars, do you? Something from the 70s?"

Chris shook her head.

"Where do you live?"

"Churchgate Street."

"That's a half-hour walk."

"I know. These bags are too heavy. If I help you home, would you consider giving me your suitcase so I can wheel my bags back?"

"Sure. But I live on Fifth, past Sainsbury's. That's a thirty-minute walk in the other direction."

Chris nodded. "I have rope in my car. We can tie the bags to the suitcase, and I'll help you wheel it home."

"And then? What happens once we get home?" Anna asked. The adrenaline had left a bitter taste in her mouth. They stood a few feet apart, but Anna knew Chris could hear the fear in her voice.

"I don't know," Chris said.

"If the worst has happened, planes will have come down…" She trailed off as she looked up at the sky. "Some people will already know that the world has changed. They might trust that the government will help, but not all will be happy to stay at home and wait it out. We need to hurry."

Together they wheeled the suitcase to Chris' car and

retrieved the rope. Anna watched as the smaller woman set to work and tied the bags to the suitcase.

"Pull," Chris instructed. "Hopefully, this will hold."

Anna pulled and the suitcase toppled over. She groaned, her lower back twinging, but she squared her jaw and pulled again.

Chris pushed, staggering as she tried to both stabilise and guide the suitcase. Leading them along the back roads she said, "If it was an…EMP? I don't think the government can fix a thing like that, can they?"

Anna wished she'd put on her running shoes. The effort of lugging a heavy suitcase around sent jolts of pain through her knee with every step. Sweat ran down her back, her shirt sticking uncomfortably to her skin. "I don't know. They must have the means to communicate. At least some of them. But even if they manage to restore pockets of power…if we can't produce food and we can't store anything perishable…" Her voice trailed off as she stopped to take a breath. "There's no water without power…how long can we last? As a functioning society?"

Behind her, Chris trailed along silently as Anna painted a potential future. "There will be looting, rioting and what have you. We could flee, but where would we go? Do you own a remote cabin somewhere? Because I reckon most of us don't." She paused, giving Chris time to answer, but the woman remained silent. "No. I think staying put is the better plan. Can you defend your home? Do you have a dog?"

"We own a house with a small garden. No dog."

"That'll be hard to defend. They can come in from all sides. Through every window. You'll have to barricade yourselves in."

"They?"

"The looters." Anna stopped to wipe her face with her shirt. "Does your husband own a gun?"

Chris snorted. "No."

Anna stopped, turned to Chris and scowled. "I'm not joking. People can survive exactly three weeks without food. With the supply chain gone, we're going to run out faster than you can imagine. There will be gangs. Mad Max-style. We don't have time to sit around and think. Don't ever hesitate, Chris. Act. You'll see. Tomorrow, life will be completely different." She resumed pulling the suitcase along and listened to the wheels wobbling along the tarmac.

After a long silence, Chris' voice almost made her jump. "I really hope you're wrong."

"Me too," Anna said, but in that moment, she would have bet a small fortune that she was right.

Unfortunately, being right meant there wouldn't be any more betting shops.

4

Chris didn't know what time it was when she made it back home. The walk to Anna's flat had been long and difficult with several large bags tied to the suitcase. Chris had waited while Anna had taken her own supplies inside. Chris' back had nearly buckled at the thought of having to carry everything up to the fourth floor. Thankfully, all of Chris' things had fit inside the suitcase, which had made the walk back a lot easier.

Chris barely recognised her street in the dark and almost missed her turning. Struggling to see without the aid of streetlights, she shuffled along the pavement to avoid the potholes. Her palms had blistered and sweat stung her hands where the skin had ripped.

Lester sat on the steps outside the front door, his face buried in his hands. With his elbows resting on his knees, he looked like he was asleep. Behind him, the door stood wide open, and Chris could see he'd lit some candles in the hallway.

She took a deep breath, her pulse pounding in her throat. "Lester?"

He jerked his head up, revealing tear-streaked cheeks. "Chris?" He reached for her with a trembling hand.

"What's happened?"

Before she could set the suitcase down, Lester grabbed her shoulders. "He's gone, Chris. Tom is gone."

Her heart leapt into her throat, and she pushed past her husband and bolted up the stairs. She heard him shouting but didn't stop to listen. She rushed into Tom's bedroom. The bed was made and had not been touched since that morning.

Her son wasn't there.

"He left to find you. I couldn't stop him."

With a painful lump in her throat and her thoughts racing she turned. "When did he leave?"

"About half an hour after the power went out. He insisted that it wasn't just a power cut. Said something was wrong, and that he had to find you and protect you."

Lester's silhouette looked pathetic the way he stood in the doorway, his shoulders slumped, his face wet and pale. Her anger spiked at the sight. "Why would he say that?"

"Something about his computers not working."

Chris' stomach flipped. So, Anna had been right. Whatever had happened had destroyed their electronics. "He's thirteen, Lester. You're his father. If you tell him not to go out in the middle of the night, he's supposed to listen."

Lester's mouth twisted into a stubborn grimace. "That's unfair, Christine." He only called her Christine when he wanted to make sure she was listening. It was his way of telling her to calm and focus, but it only made her angrier. "Should I have physically restrained him? Punched him if he didn't listen? What do you think I should have done? I told him to wait. I told him you had security at the shop. He didn't listen."

Her bubbling anger threatened to spill over as her husband spoke. Useless. He was useless. Couldn't keep his job. Couldn't keep their son safe. "You could have locked the door and gone with him. You're his father," Chris said through clenched teeth.

Lester seemed to deflate at the venom in her tone. He suddenly looked old, his receding hairline greying at the edges. "I was worried about you. What if you'd come home, and we had both been gone? The phones aren't working."

"You could have left a note." Her eyes narrowed to slits. "You're useless, you know. Useless as a father, useless as a husband. Sometimes I wish you'd just—"

"What, Christine?" He crossed his arms in front of his chest. The expression on his face dared her to say something cruel, but his arms gave away that he was bracing himself because he fully expected her to do so. Because that's who she was. The woman who said cruel things. "What is it you were going to say?"

"Sometimes I wish you'd just give up and end it all," she whispered, regretting the words as soon as they'd left her mouth, even more so when his shoulders slumped in defeat. "I'm going to find Tom."

She went back downstairs, pointing at the bags and suitcase. "I don't think it's just a power cut either. I've brought supplies. How about you put them away while I go back to the shop and look for Tom."

"Shouldn't I come with you?"

Her heart seized in her chest. After everything she'd just said to him, his first thought was still to stay with her and protect her. She didn't deserve that. Didn't deserve him.

"Just put the food away." Tears stung her eyes as she grabbed her pepper spray. Lester had bought it for her, worried about her walking from her car to the hospital when she worked the night shift. It wasn't legal to carry pepper spray in England, and she didn't know (or didn't *care* to know) how he'd bought it, but she always kept a can on her.

She dropped it into her handbag before retrieving a steak knife from the cutlery drawer in the kitchen.

Lester stood in the hallway, jaw squared, upper body taut, but completely silent as she shuffled past him. She couldn't bear to look at him and closed the front door behind her, the scent of his aftershave filling her with remorse.

She had to focus on Tom now. She had to find her son.

That was all that mattered.

This time, she walked along the main road. She cursed. Had she been at Anna's when he'd reached Tesco?

Would she have come across him if she'd followed the main road?

Why hadn't he come back home? What if something had happened to him?

What if he'd gone to the hospital? It was easy to mix up her shifts.

Instinctively, she reached into her bag, fumbling for her phone, then remembered that it no longer worked.

How parents brought up children without mobile phones had been baffling her ever since Tom had been old enough to leave the house without her. The thought of letting him go in the mornings and telling him to come back before supper without being able to check in on him transformed her stomach into a ball of anxiety.

Without the noise of the traffic, Harlow had been plunged into an eerie stillness. Twinkling stars lit up the sky, but without the streetlights, it was too dark for her to make out the pavement on the other side of the road.

Clutching her bag to herself, Chris strode down the middle of the road, turning her head from left to right and back again as if she were sitting centre court at Wimbledon.

Her back hurt. She'd been awake for almost twenty-four hours and had spent most of those hours on her feet.

Something on the pavement to her left caught her attention and she stopped, furrowing her brows. It looked like a pile of clothes. Narrowing her eyes, she realised it was a person.

About to rush over, Chris bit her lip. What if it was a trap?

She'd read about this on the Internet. People who stopped on empty country roads thinking there had been an accident and somebody needed their help, only to be tackled and robbed.

Sometimes killed.

But she was a nurse, and this person might need her help. She slid her hand into her bag and fumbled for her pepper spray. Holding it in her right hand, she crossed the road and knelt. The tarmac dug into her knees, shredding her tights.

It was an old man with neatly combed short, grey hair. She gingerly pushed on his shoulder and rolled him onto his back. Definitely not homeless, Chris thought, taking in his appearance. He was wearing smart trousers and a shirt. A walking stick was lying beside him. She noticed a deep gash on his forehead. The surrounding skin was caked with dried blood.

He must have fallen hours ago.

She reached for his neck and placed two fingers against the cold skin. "Sir? Can you hear me?" Moving her hand to his nose, she sighed.

He was dead.

She searched his pockets for a wallet when she noticed the wristband indicating that he wore a pacemaker.

She reached for her phone. This time she remembered it was dead before rummaging through her bag and slapped her forehead with her palm. "Damn."

How many times would she do this before she remembered without even trying?

Electronics were dead. There was no power.

And no ambulances.

His skin appeared grey in the bright moonlight.

Had he died because of his pacemaker? Had the—she scratched her head. What had Anna called it? An EMP? Had that killed him?

She looked around. There was no one nearby.

It was after midnight, and, just like Anna had predicted, most people seemed to have gone to bed. What else was there to do?

That's what Chris would have done if she hadn't met Anna.

She closed the dead man's eyes gently and murmured, "Where did you live?" She briefly considered knocking on doors, but she had to find Tom first.

If the man was still there after she'd found Tom, she'd figure something out, but hopefully he'd be someone else's problem by then.

She ran the last mile to the shop. Sweat trickled down her temples and neck. She came to a stop in the carpark near the entrance. Panting, she bent over, leaning her hands on her legs and waited for her breathing to slow.

She heard a cry and spotted movement close to where she'd parked her car.

Tom!

Two figures were struggling with each other. She recognised her son's t-shirt. Tom stood with his back pressed against the side of her Volvo, kicking his attacker who had one hand pressed over Tom's mouth. Tom's sweat-stained shirt smeared the window as he stumbled.

"Tom?"

Tom kicked again, then bit down on the hand still on his face. Chris took a step forward and smacked the back of the man's head with her handbag. He spun around and she raised her pepper spray.

It was Mike.

"Mike! What are you doing?"

"Oh. Look who's back." He sneered, rubbing the back of his head where she'd hit him. With his taser still aimed at Tom, he spat at her feet. "This is what happens to the son of a thief."

Despite the darkness, Chris saw the fear on her son's face. She mouthed, "It'll be okay," her eyes never leaving the taser.

"Have you come back to rob us again?" Mike asked. "Your son didn't believe me when I said you'd been fired because you were caught stealing. He said I was a dirty liar. Didn't you, Tom?" Mike snarled like a wild animal, the veins along his throat bulging with anger.

Chris' pulse pounded loudly in her ears, and she had to strain to understand Mike's words. "You're threatening my son with an illegal taser, Mike. He's thirteen." She struggled to speak, her voice shaking with anger. "Do you remember that lawsuit I promised you? It's just got a lot worse."

"I don't think there'll be any lawsuit," Mike replied. "I think it's everyone for themselves. You're a thief. And he's a thief's son."

"And you're the new sheriff in town?" Chris swung her handbag a second time, but Mike ducked and turned. "Let him go you dirty—"

She stopped, staring at the taser now aimed at her, then emptied her pepper spray into his eyes.

Blinded, Mike screamed, clutching at his face with one hand. The other held onto the taser, and he pulled the trigger.

Chris squeezed her eyes shut, preparing for the painful shock.

Nothing happened.

She blinked, opened one eye.

He'd aimed it straight at her.

It should have knocked her to the ground. Reduced her to a whimpering heap.

Tears streamed down his face, and rage twisted his mouth into an ugly grimace as he staggered towards her, hands outstretched, trying to tackle her.

She threw the empty can at him and pulled out her knife. Her hand had stopped trembling and she felt calm, focused. She moved forward, buried the knife into Mike's stomach. It slid into his soft plump flesh like a hot knife through butter.

Fascinated, she watched the blade disappear to the hilt and swallowed.

She'd crossed the line.

Red bloomed around the knife's hilt and a softness replaced the fury in Mike's brown eyes. A look she'd seen many times as a nurse.

The look of a man who knew he was dying.

She could pay for the food she'd taken; she couldn't undo this.

Self-defence or not. She had wilfully taken a life.

He clutched the knife with both hands as though wanting to pull it out, but instead he dropped to his knees with a gentle gasp. Cold sweat dotted his hairline as the life drained from him the way it drained from most people: quietly.

"Mum?"

Chris flinched. She'd forgotten about Tom. Her son stared at her with wide eyes, and she took his hand, squeezed it. "We need to go home, sweetie."

"But your car—"

"It's not working, Tom. I thought you'd figured that out."

His eyes were glued to the dying man writhing on the ground. His jaw hung open as though he wanted to scream.

In only a few hours, the world had changed.

And her son, who had only just learned to live in the old world, would have to learn a whole new way of life.

It would be hard, but she would guide him.

Anna had been right. There was no time to hesitate. No time to think.

She had to act.

Chris bent over Mike and grabbed her knife. As she stood over his lifeless body, hatred bubbled up in her gut, and she felt strangely powerful. She twisted the knife before pulling it out. Wiping the blade on Mike's shirt, she looked up at Tom. "Are you ready?"

She concealed the knife in her bag. Tossed the taser into the bin.

Tom stared and didn't blink. Just stood next to her Volvo as if paralysed.

"Tom?"

"Shouldn't we…don't we have to call the police?"

"How?"

He blinked, his eyes slowly focusing on her as though seeing her for the first time. "I don't know. What's going on?"

Chris patted his shoulder and gave him a grim smile. Soon, he'd be taller than her. Even taller than Lester. "I don't know, sweetie, but something bad has happened and the world has changed. We need to adapt fast."

She stepped over Mike's body without giving it another look and pulled on Tom's elbow. "Come on. Your dad is waiting for us at home."

Yes. The world had changed, and they needed to adapt. *I hope you're wrong,* she'd said to Anna only a few hours ago, but now everything was different.

If the world hadn't changed, she'd be in a lot of trouble come morning.

And just like that, Chris was hoping for the worst.

5

Anna set down a bowl of kibble, and Oreo gobbled it up with the enthusiasm of a dog who didn't know the world had changed and that one day soon they would run out of kibble.

Her gaze drifted to the batteries lying on the dining room table and she frowned. She had no idea how quickly the radio would drain them, or how long she would need them for, but she remembered reading in an article once that removing the batteries after every use would make them last longer.

She'd waited an entire day before trying to turn on the radio, afraid that it had been damaged beyond repair along with all the other electronic devices. Afraid that she'd be truly alone, cut off from the world. But mostly, she'd been afraid to hear that the world had changed. That she had been right after all.

Anna preferred avoiding problems and pretending they weren't there. She would always hope they'd disappear if she ignored them for long enough.

The morning after the power cut, she'd heard shouting outside. Opening the window, she'd glimpsed police officers with megaphones telling people the shops were closed for the time being and to stay inside.

The first time Anna had put the batteries in the radio, she'd taken them straight out again and placed the radio back into its box. The second time, she'd reached for her phone to google the BBC's broadcast frequency, only to remember that her phone was dead.

The third time, she'd scanned for stations, finding nothing but static. Sitting at her table, she'd buried her face in her hands.

What now?

She'd decided to scan for stations twice a day—once in the morning and once in the evening to preserve the batteries.

Then, to keep busy and to feel more in control, she'd proceeded to portion her food into daily rations of a thousand calories each.

Thankfully, she wasn't particularly tall, and a thousand calories daily would sustain her for a while. If she lost too much weight, she'd add peanut butter and olive oil to her meals.

She couldn't starve herself, couldn't allow herself to grow weak and tired. She needed to be strong to survive the coming months.

Humans could survive three weeks without food, but once they began to starve, they'd become desperate. Dangerous.

Feral.

She had to hide and wait it out.

Anna stuffed her rations into freezer bags, making small, orderly packets which she hid behind her clothes in her wardrobe—just in case looters broke into her flat.

Once finished, she counted the packets. She had enough food for at least three months. Rice and baked beans weren't an exciting diet, but they would allow her to stay put if nothing else. If she adhered to the thousand calories a day rule, she might even last four months without having to try and find more food.

What worried her more was water. She'd filled every glass, every bottle and every jug in the house until the tap began spluttering and spitting brown sludge into her sink. Together with the bottles she'd taken from Tesco, she had sixty litres of fresh water.

This was England. Hopefully, there'd be some rain. She'd collect it in her recycling bin and boil it over an open flame.

But where?

Once the rioting and looting began, she'd have to avoid the balcony for fear of someone spotting the flat being occupied.

"Or do we want them to know that we're at home? As a deterrent?" she asked Oreo, rubbing the nape of her neck. Both an empty flat and a flat occupied by a single woman sounded like an open invitation to her ears.

She sighed and glanced outside. The sky was a pale blue. Not a cloud in sight. Perhaps she'd be lucky, and it would rain in the next few days.

Oreo sat on his bed, grooming his paws, and Anna sat down on the tiled floor next to him. She buried her hand in his fur, her fingers disappearing in his thick, long coat. "You and me against the world, eh? Who would have thought?"

One day everything had been normal, and the next…

"I miss the Internet." Oreo continued to lick his paws, ears pricked in her direction. "And the library."

Oreo grumbled, then yawned.

"I'm glad you're a bit lazy," she mumbled, tickling the paw he'd stretched out towards her. His leg twitched and he pulled it away. "Sometimes I think your dad must have been a cat. Your last walk was two days ago. Most Border Collies would be eating my sofa by now."

Oreo enjoyed accompanying her on runs and tolerated

walks, but he *loved* chasing after a tennis ball. As long as he had his yellow ball, he was a happy dog.

But he also liked to nap.

When it rained especially, he would nap all day long.

Anna heard muffled shouting outside.

"What the—" She stood, walked over to her kitchen window and peered outside. Oreo growled with his black ears pricked.

Two soldiers were talking to a police officer in the middle of the road. They were wearing helmets and had assault rifles strapped to their chests. The police officer was gesticulating with both hands.

Anna opened the window, but a strong breeze swallowed their words.

She reached for the radio and inserted the batteries with trembling hands. Sitting down, she searched for the BBC, tapping her foot against the chair.

What if—

No. She wouldn't allow the voice in her mind to come to the forefront. Wouldn't allow it to scare her. She'd left it behind when she moved out. Left it back in her childhood home. Left it with her father where it belonged.

She wouldn't listen to it.

She had to focus.

Her heart fluttered when the static turned into a real voice. A man who spoke in concerned tones. She immediately pictured a middle-aged professor with small, round glasses and a neatly trimmed beard. They'd chosen their speaker well.

He spoke slowly, enunciating every word as though his life depended on it.

She narrowed her eyes, focusing on what he was saying.

"…are working as quickly as we can. The government and the army are asking for your trust and your patience, and most importantly, they are asking for your cooperation. Every UK citizen will receive their fair share of food, water and medicine. No one will be left behind. For now, in order to make sure that our streets stay safe, everyone has to remain inside."

"I don't think we'll be allowed outside anytime soon," she said to Oreo. Her pulse thundered in her ears as anxiety crept from her stomach into her throat.

She'd thought of riots and looting. She'd thought of fighting in the streets and in the supermarkets. She'd been waiting for the government to step in, but she hadn't considered the army patrolling the streets.

She hadn't considered not being *allowed* outside. The army stepping in. Taking control. Stripping England's citizens of their freedom in a desperate attempt to control the situation and secure supplies.

"Together with trusted charities and corporations, the councils are working as quickly as they can to restore the national grid."

Anna turned to Oreo who was licking his empty bowl and frowned. "What a load of bollocks," she muttered. "They're not being honest. I get it. They don't want us to panic, but without power…"

She sighed.

She looked outside where one of the armed soldiers was holding a megaphone up to his mouth. Placing her elbows on the windowsill, she listened.

"In the meantime, every household will receive their fair share of food and water, and we ask those of you who have enough supplies for the moment to…" his voice droned on, but Anna had heard enough.

The message would no doubt be played on a loop.

A message that didn't mention how long it would take to restore the power. Not even an estimate. Not even a guess.

No information about the cause of all of this and what had actually happened.

They either didn't want the public to know, or they simply didn't have a clue.

"Once a week we will distribute supply crates. To receive your crates, please sign up to the Government Food Supply Scheme tomorrow morning."

Anna rubbed her forehead, smoothing her frown with her fingers. Would they be inspecting homes before they handed out supplies? Or could she pretend not to have anything and be given more water?

Did they even have the necessary manpower to search homes?

"I wish Sarah were here," she said to Oreo, closing the window. It had taken the army almost three days to mobilise.

Had Sarah left her home? Was she on her way to Harlow?

Or had she done the same as Anna had and stayed put?

"How am I ever going to find you?" she whispered to the photograph sitting next to the urn containing her mother's ashes. Anna walked over and traced the photograph with her finger. Her father had taken it almost fifteen years ago. Both her mother and Sarah were smiling in it. Her sister had only been seventeen. By that point, Anna had already moved out.

They hadn't expected their mother to die only three years later.

On her deathbed, Anna had promised her to take care of Sarah.

"Always," she'd said, squeezing her mother's hand.

What if she couldn't keep her promise?

No. She wouldn't allow the voice inside her head to take over and fill her with worry. Oreo tilted his head, his black eyes watching her.

The man on the radio had said that everyone must remain inside. Was that even legal?

Then again, it hadn't been legal for Anna to take three months' worth of food from Tesco without paying.

Theft.

She was a thief.

You don't seem to have a lot of sense, Anna. The lump in her throat grew, and she closed her eyes, pushing back against her father's voice. *Hopefully, I can change that before it's too late.*

"No!" She flinched hearing her own voice. Oreo whined, bumping her thigh with his nose as though reminding her that he was right there.

Her support. But she needed more than just a dog. "Sarah," she said to Oreo. "We need to find Sarah."

How did the army communicate?

They had to communicate somehow.

Perhaps one of the soldiers outside could help her. If they had radios.

If only she knew what had happened. What kind of electronics had survived. Pinching the bridge of her nose, she considered the possibilities. Again.

She'd done nothing but consider the possibilities for the last two days. Sitting on her bed, hugging her knees into her chest. Paralysed by fear. By the unknown. She'd considered the possibilities over and over again.

Had it been the sun? If another country had attacked, the army wouldn't be standing in the streets talking about food and water.

They'd be busy fighting.

Unless…unless the entirety of Europe was under attack.

Unless the fight was happening somewhere else.

She buried her face in her hands and groaned. Perhaps one of the soldiers in the street would be able to shed some light on the situation.

"Wait here," she said to Oreo and slid into her flip flops.

The air in the stairwell was cooler than inside her flat. An almost agreeable temperature.

It was a small block with only four flats.

The couple who lived right below her didn't seem to be home. She hadn't heard any noise coming from their flat since the power had gone out. She pressed her ear against the door and listened.

Nothing.

They had to be away.

Anna heard the child from the ground floor screaming all the way up from the third floor, seemingly in the middle of a tantrum. The soothing voice of a mother replied, progressively growing louder.

The door to the flat on the second floor stood open a crack. A bald man stuck his head outside, a scowl on his face. He wasn't wearing a shirt and absentmindedly scratched his hairy chest. Spotting Anna, he grimaced. "All right?"

She nodded. "Trying to see if I can talk to one of the soldiers in the street."

His scowl deepened. "Trying to sell yourself for food? Think you can get more than the rest of us?"

She stared, blinked slowly. Almost laughed. Then she shook her head. "No," she mumbled. Blood rushed to her head, making her blush. She didn't know what else to say and dashed down the stairs instead, past the empty flat on the first floor. The letting agency had been in the process of finding new tenants.

Outside, the sun was beating down on the tarmac. The soldier who'd spoken earlier was standing by the traffic lights speaking with his partner. He barely looked older than eighteen. Anna winced, realising she was old enough to be his mother. Surely, he could be reasoned with?

The warm air was thick with humidity and the pungent smell of baking tarmac filled her nose. Her flat would warm up fast now. By mid-July it would be unbearable, and this time she had no ice, no cold water and no fan. Worse, she'd have to drink more water to make up for the fluids she lost through sweating.

"Excuse me, madam, you have to stay inside."

Anna scowled. She hated being called madam. It always gave her the impression that they were addressing someone else. Her mother, or somebody behind her. They couldn't possibly mean her because she wasn't old enough to be called madam.

You're approaching forty, she reminded herself. And the soldier stalking towards her wasn't even old enough to grow a proper beard.

She smiled at the blond shadow on his upper lip. "I just want to ask you a few questions." She suddenly wished she'd put on some make-up and brushed her hair. After three days without a shower, she realised she must look a state.

Then again, what could the world possibly expect from her in such circumstances?

Now the soldier stood in front of her, she didn't know where to start.

"If this is about the supplies," the soldier started, clutching his rifle with a white-knuckled grip. His left eye twitched as he spoke. "We will begin—"

"My sister is in Colchester."

He moved his head as though suppressing the urge to roll his eyes. "A lot of people have family in various places."

"I know. I was just wondering if there was any way I could get a message to her via you. You must have the means to communicate, don't you?"

"We're not the post office. We're here to ensure that everyone gets their fair share of food and that our streets are safe while the government works on restoring the power."

"Are there any—"

"I can't help you." His features hardened, and his narrowed eyes grew sharp. "Are you in urgent need of food and water?"

"No." Anna shook her head. She had to get through to him somehow. She had to make him listen. "Why are you following these orders instead of looking after your own family?" She paused and waited for her words to sink in. "Are they prepared for the coming famine? Are they safe?"

He frowned and cocked his head as though considering her words. Letting go of the rifle strapped to his chest, he scratched behind his ear.

"They're not going to restore the power anytime soon," she continued. "Everything's gone bust. And once food runs out, you won't be able to keep the peace."

"I know how to do my job, madam."

"I don't doubt that for a second. At least for now. But once people are starving?" She licked her lip, contemplating her next words. "Look—what's your name?"

"That is none of your business, *madam*. Nobody will be starving. We are handling it. Please go back inside, and please refrain from spreading any rumours."

His words sounded robotic as if he were repeating a mantra he'd been given by his superiors.

Not easily discouraged, Anna tried again. "Without power, nobody can produce food. And without power, the food we've already produced will spoil. We're probably already running out of everything fresh, and by the end of July we'll be fighting over tinned goods. Do you understand what I'm saying?"

He shrugged. "If you say so. Please go back inside."

He'd been given a mantra, and he'd been told not to engage.

Anna sighed. "Our society depends on electricity."

His tone shifted, and his hand was back on his rifle. "Please go back inside."

"The reason the army is out on the streets is so that the government can stockpile food while we're prisoners inside our own homes. The rich and powerful get to survive a little bit longer than the rest of us."

He raised his rifle, not quite pointing it at her, but his intentions were clear. "Go back inside."

This time, he'd dropped the please. Anna was about to give up when she noticed her second-floor neighbour approaching. He wore jogging trousers and had put on an oversized shirt with a sloth printed across the front. She could make out the word coffee, but the letters folded over his beer-belly, and she struggled to read the font.

"Sir, you have to get back inside." This time the soldier levelled his rifle at the newcomer straight away. Anna glimpsed a flicker of fear in his brown eyes, but it was quickly replaced by determination.

The other soldier was still standing by the traffic lights, busy with his megaphone, but he was looking over now. "Do you need help, John?"

"I'm fine," John shouted, gritting his teeth. "Sir, please go back inside."

Her neighbour rubbed his bald head. Sweat dotted his temples. "My mother lives on the other side of Harlow, and you can't stop me from visiting her. She's old and sick, and she depends on me looking in on her. I don't think you lot get to decide whether or not I can see her."

"Your mother will be taken care of, I promise. I'll personally make sure—"

The man cut him off with a sneer. "I'm going now. You won't shoot me. This is England, not Venezuela."

Anna reached out to pull him back with her, then remembered the way he'd barked at her in the stairwell.

"Go back inside, madam," John said to her. He gave her a long, almost pleading look before turning his attention back to the bald man. He pursed his lips, his left eye twitching.

Anna didn't doubt he'd shoot.

She didn't know her neighbours. She avoided bumping into them whenever she could. She knew the couple who lived below her spent a lot of time abroad, and she knew the family on the ground floor had a noisy toddler who threw the occasional tantrum. The father was a young man who worked the night shift at the local pharmacy while studying to become an IT specialist. She'd bumped into him once, and they'd exchanged a few words. Anna had never met his wife, had only seen her from behind.

She wasn't a fan of small talk. She never knew what to say. Hated the neighbourly chit chat that seemed appropriate when meeting in the stairwell. She'd never even seen the man from the second floor prior to this day.

Nausea washed over her as she watched him walk up the road towards Sainsbury's. Away from the two soldiers.

Anna knew they had their orders, and if they didn't stand up to people like him, they'd have riots on their hands before long.

And they definitely had permission to shoot.

Besides, there'd be no repercussions. Without smartphones and without the Internet, nobody would know. There'd be no videos. No social media posts to go viral.

And right now, people had much bigger problems than police brutality.

Law and order was more important than a human life.

They wouldn't risk anything by shooting this man. On the contrary, the street would cower.

And obey.

And that's exactly what they wanted.

Strength was found in numbers, and without the Internet,

without communication, people were alone. They certainly *felt* alone.

Anna shuffled back inside. She stopped by the front door and watched as her neighbour approached the roundabout.

"I'm warning you one last time," John commanded. His voice shook ever so slightly, but the grip on his rifle looked steady.

Bracing herself, Anna shielded her face with her hands and turned away from the road.

"I'm going to see my mother, and you can't stop—"

A single shot rang out.

Anna squeezed her eyes shut. Standing at the bottom of the stairs, she trembled, her hands gripping the bannister. She waited. Waited for her heart to stop thumping in her chest. Waited for her tears to stop falling.

It wasn't until she heard Oreo bark that she went back upstairs.

When she glanced out of her kitchen window a few hours later, the body had been removed, and nothing but dark marks in the middle of the road near the roundabout remained.

She spotted the soldiers sitting by the traffic lights and frowned.

John was gone.

He'd been replaced by a stocky woman with sharp cheekbones and an angular jaw.

Anna wondered if the young man had listened to her, after all, or if his superiors were following standard procedure.

She closed the window and let out a long breath.

Tomorrow, she'd knock on the bald man's flat and find out if he'd had a wife. If not, she'd ask the neighbours on the ground floor if they wanted to split his supplies.

But for now, Anna sat down with her back pressed against the wall in her bedroom, her hands stroking Oreo for comfort.

6

As Chris stood in the doorway to Tom's bedroom, studying the back of her teenage son's head, his dark hair curling around his ears and neck, it occurred to her that life was unfair.

No one ever got what they deserved.

And if they did, it was by chance.

Her son deserved safety and love. He deserved to grow up and find a partner, have his own family. He deserved to party and travel, explore the world.

He didn't deserve this new world with soldiers in the streets and the threat of starvation looming.

Chris' mind reeled. It hadn't stopped spinning since she'd met Anna. Scattered thoughts clouded her mind.

She'd forced herself to sit still, make a list. An inventory. A plan.

She'd forced herself to ignore the outside world. Anna had been right. They needed to hunker down. Wait it out.

Play dead until the predator had moved on.

But who or what was the predator? And how long would they need to hunker down for?

Three days ago, the army had shown up and promised to

distribute supplies. Armed with megaphones and assault rifles, they patrolled the streets in a desperate attempt to keep the peace.

There were five stages of grief: denial, anger, bargaining, depression, acceptance.

Chris assumed most people were still in denial.

Denial meant thinking that everything would go back to normal. Soon. The government would look after them and fix everything. Denial meant that life as they knew it wasn't over. That they were still living in a safe world.

They simply had to stay at home and wait it out.

Chris knew better. Torn between anger, bargaining and depression, she sighed. She wondered how long it would take before people progressed from denial to anger. How long it would take people to understand that they were running out of food, and the government couldn't fix anything.

Every man for himself, Mike had said. Her manager hadn't deserved to die, but Chris felt no remorse. She'd expected to wake up feeling nauseous, racked with guilt.

Instead she'd woken up feeling proud. She'd saved her son. She'd looked after her family.

She had a chance to survive this.

The night before had been her first shift at the hospital since the power had gone out. "Is the hospital even still open?" Lester had asked. "I'm not comfortable with you out there."

Without the phones working, she'd had no way of contacting work. She'd gone outside, holding her NHS badge like a shield, and a soldier had handed her a bright orange armband. "Keep that visible at all times. It identifies you as medical personnel," he'd instructed, and she'd nodded, her heart thumping in her chest.

At the hospital, they'd welcomed her with hugs and disgusting, cold coffee. Half the staff hadn't shown up.

Nobody knew if they lived too far away or if they were too scared to come into work.

Or if they simply thought work no longer mattered.

In the emergency department, dozens of patients had waited for medical attention.

"We should pull up staff records. See if we can coordinate with the army to find more doctors and nurses," Chris had proposed.

"We've tried that. I sent Hannah to the archives on Tuesday, but it looks like everything's electronic these days," one of the doctors had replied.

The shift had been chaotic. With no imaging and no power, they couldn't do much more than provide basic emergency medicine. Some of the doctors and nurses had spouted conspiracy theories, discussing everything from aliens and the Rapture to a nuclear attack.

It had been a long night.

Chris clasped her hand over her mouth and stifled a yawn.

Tom turned his head, spotted her and frowned. "Mum? I didn't know you were back from the hospital." There were deep, dark circles around his eyes, and he looked as if he hadn't slept in days.

"Good morning, sweetie," she said with a smile.

"When am I allowed outside again? I want to see James."

Chris watched as Tom ran a hand through his thick, tousled hair, pulling on a few strands. She scratched below her ear, considering her next words. Like all nurses, she had some basic understanding of psychology. It wasn't uncommon for a patient to grow increasingly anxious and sometimes even become aggressive while waiting for treatment.

But dealing with teenagers and their hormonal mood swings was different.

Tom and James had been inseparable for almost a decade.

"Can I come in?"

Tom nodded, and Chris sat down in his desk chair, careful not to invade his space. He'd used to love hugging and kissing her until he was ten years old, then one day he'd just stopped.

"It's weird, isn't it?" she asked quietly.

He nodded. Peach fuzz covered his chin and upper lip, and the first few angry spots dotted his jawline. Soon, Lester would have to teach him how to shave, and yet it felt as though it was only yesterday that Tom had been a little baby.

"How come you're allowed to go to work, and I'm not allowed outside?" His voice was calm, devoid of anger. It wasn't an accusation. He was simply trying to understand a world in which soldiers patrolled the streets.

"I'm an essential worker. The hospital is there to save people's lives. You just want to visit your mates. One is a priority, and the other isn't. Does that make sense?"

He shrugged.

"They're expecting riots and looting. There's only one way to keep us quiet, and it's by keeping us trapped inside our homes."

Tom frowned and placed the book he'd been reading on his pillow. C++. *Another* programming language. It was all he read these days.

He scooted closer towards Chris. "They're expecting riots?"

Chris realised she'd been wrong to assume Tom would be aware of the seriousness of the situation. When he talked about computers and game development, he seemed all grown up. For a moment, she'd forgotten that he was only thirteen years old.

"We only have a certain amount of food, water and medicine in the UK," she explained, wishing she could put an arm around him. "Some of what we use we import from other countries, and the rest we produce ourselves. Production needs machinery. Machinery needs electricity. To import supplies, we need lorries and as you know, cars and lorries no longer work. Besides, if this has happened not just to us but to other countries as well, they can't produce anything either."

"Does that mean we'll starve?"

She bit back a *yes*. Of course that's what was about to happen, but there was no need to scare Tom. "It's important right now that everything is being distributed fairly, and that everyone uses only as much as they need. If everyone takes only what they need to survive, we will be able to save more people."

"But we have enough money to buy—"

"Imagine if only people with money were able to stock up on supplies. That wouldn't be fair, would it? Just because some people are poor doesn't mean they deserve to starve."

"But—"

She glowered at him, and he stopped talking, pulling his mouth into a defiant pout.

"Besides," Chris continued, "with your father having lost his job and being dependent solely on my salary, we'll run out of money sooner rather than later. If this had happened in another two to three months, we wouldn't have been able to buy any supplies. Do you think we deserve to starve in three months?"

"No."

"So, why do you believe people deserve to starve today?"

"Why does the government get to decide who gets what and how much?" He'd avoided her question, but his features had softened. A pensive look had fallen over his face.

"They've been elected. Put in charge of running the country. It's their job." Chris smiled. "Why, who would you put in charge?"

"I don't know."

"Well, somebody has to decide."

He reached for his book and flicked through the pages, pressing his lips together. After a moment of silence, he looked up at her. "Mum?"

"Yes?"

"Why did Dad lose his job? He won't talk to me about it."

Chris pulled her knees up to her chest, swivelling in the chair and sighed. Her thoughts drifted back to the night the world had gone dark, and what she'd said to Lester before leaving.

She swallowed.

Sometimes I wish—

When they'd come home, Lester had embraced Tom, then placed a kiss on top of her head. She could have sworn he'd looked as if he had aged five years during the few hours she'd been gone.

They'd all sat down at the kitchen table and discussed what had happened.

Chris only said that she'd found Tom waiting by her car.

"The security guard wouldn't let me inside the shop," Tom said and left it at that. He didn't mention to Lester that Chris had killed her manager. In fact, he didn't mention Mike at all.

"Why did you come looking for me?" Chris asked, and Tom explained to his parents why he thought it had been an EMP and what that meant. "My iPad, my iPhone and my laptop wouldn't turn on," he said.

They discussed the possibility of an attack either by a foreign nation or terrorists.

"It could have been the sun," Lester said. "It's happened once before. It's called the Carrington Event. Back then, telegraph systems failed. It would be a lot worse today because the entire world depends on electricity."

After Tom had gone to bed, Chris and Lester checked on him. Hand in hand they stood in his doorway and watched his chest rise and fall slowly.

"I'm sorry," she whispered, and Lester squeezed her hand. She was the woman who said cruel things, and Lester was the man who always forgave her.

"Mum?" her son's voice pulled her back to the present and she sighed.

"Dad is ill."

"I know," Tom said. "He has depression. James said his uncle killed himself because of depression. Will Dad—"

"No!" Chris shook her head. "Your dad will get better."

"Why wasn't his boss more understanding?"

"I don't know. Depression makes it awfully hard to focus. It drains you, and your dad wasn't able to do his job."

Tom frowned, contemplating her words. "How was your shift? Are you still able to do your job?"

"It's hard to work without technology. I'd never realised how much we depend on it. We can't do any x-rays. No CTs. No proper lighting."

"Doesn't the hospital have generators?" Tom asked.

"We do. But most of our machinery is toast."

His eyes lit up and he straightened, scooting even closer. "Could you smuggle one home?"

"A generator?" Chris blinked. "What for?"

"Some of the small appliances might still work. I could recharge my batteries. We could look for working electronics. In a warehouse for example." In his excitement, the words tumbled from his mouth so fast, she had to concentrate hard to catch them all.

"Is that even possible?" Chris asked. "Dad said this could have been caused by the sun."

"It's possible." Tom nodded. "But I think there'd be

flashes in the sky. It may have been too cloudy when it happened.

"Wouldn't NASA have known about this?"

"Perhaps they didn't realise how bad it would be."

"Is there any way for us to figure out what's caused this for certain?"

"I don't think so. Not unless someone tells us."

Chris pinched the bridge of her nose. "But you believe we can find working electronics?"

"Your torch still works. So, yes. But without generators, electronics won't be much use."

"Interesting." Chris smiled. Pride filled her at the sight of her son. He'd always loved technology and had learned how to build and take apart computers with Lester's help. At eleven, he'd taught himself how to program a simple app.

"Mum? How are you staying so calm?"

"I don't know, sweetie. Living without electricity is bizarre and surreal, but for now it's okay."

"For now," Tom said softly.

Chris sighed. "I think it's going to get a lot worse, and it'll get a lot worse quickly, but I believe we can deal with it. I believe we can survive this by working together." A lie for the benefit of her teenage son. Life wasn't fair. Nobody got what they deserved. Her grandmother had believed that the universe never gave you more than you could handle, but Chris didn't know how to handle any of this.

Then again, she remembered Anna's words: *There will be gangs. Mad Max-style. We don't have the time to sit around and think. Don't ever hesitate. Act.*

And she'd acted. She'd protected her son. She'd proven that she was strong.

Chris wondered if she had enough planks of wood in the shed to barricade the windows. They had to protect their home from the inevitable looting once people's supplies had run out. The biggest danger out there would be desperate people. People she'd once considered neighbours.

It would be hard to defend the house. You could get in through the backdoor, through the side-door, and through any of the windows on the ground floor.

A smaller space like Anna's flat for example was much easier to defend, but Anna didn't have a garden to plant vegetables.

She slowly rose to her feet and yawned. She hadn't slept in over a day. "I'm going to sleep for a few hours."

She walked to the door when Tom's voice stopped her. "Mum?"

Fear laced his voice, and she swallowed. "Yes?"

"That man you hurt outside of Tesco…"

Her stomach dropped. She'd expected this question. She'd dreaded it. "Mike," she whispered.

"What happened? Why did he attack us?"

"Mike was an awful man. A horrible manager. He didn't care for his employees. I'm sorry he died, but he threatened both you and me."

"But why?"

"I was…" She scratched her head. "I was trying to get things for us. Things we'd need like food and medicine. I just took it. It might have been wrong, but I took it. I told him that I would pay for it the next day. I told him to take the same for his own family. He wouldn't listen. He said I was trying to steal from Tesco."

Tom frowned. "But…"

"The tills were inoperable, Tom. With no power…we couldn't scan the items. We couldn't pay."

"Oh." He smacked his forehead. "Of course."

She thought back to Mike's pale face. The way he'd lain next to her car with his eyes wide open and devoid of life, staring into nothingness.

"I work there. It's not like I could have disappeared into thin air, right? He knew the phones weren't working. He knew something was wrong, but he insisted that I couldn't take home any supplies. Roland, our security guard, he let me go. Mike tried to attack me, and Roland punched him."

"Wow." Tom grinned in that way boys did when they heard a story involving a fist fight. She smiled, watching his eyes twinkle as he moved his body, punching the air with his fist, imagining the scene.

"When I came home, Dad told me you'd gone to find me, and I went back for you. Mike was threatening you, and he knew I'd taken home supplies. I couldn't risk him coming after us. I don't know if killing him was the right thing to do but he knew where we live, and he was threatening our family."

"Thanks for explaining, Mum." Tom nodded thoughtfully. "Are they going to arrest you?"

"I don't think so. There were a lot of injured people at the hospital last night. Some had clashed with patrolling soldiers. Others had been hurt in the fires." She thought of the old man she'd found collapsed in the street. How many had died in their beds, their pacemakers failing? "I don't think they'll be looking for me, and it's not like they can check CCTV. Do you have any other questions?"

Tom shook his head and turned his attention back to his programming book. Chris left his room, closing the door behind her.

It was early still, and grey clouds filled the skies of Harlow with misery. She was exhausted. There was so much to do, but she wouldn't be able to do anything without a rest. A quick nap, then she'd see if she was able to grow anything in their garden.

Chris pushed the door to the master bedroom open and stepped inside.

She froze.

Lester was lying on top of the covers, the bed untouched from when she'd made it the previous morning. At first glance, it looked as though he was asleep, but she immediately knew something was wrong.

Fear snaked up her spine.

His skin was too pale, almost grey.

Blood trickled from his slashed wrists, soaking the white sheets. A razor blade rested in his right palm, the sharp edge caked with drying blood.

Chris placed both of her hands over her mouth. She swayed, lost her balance and tumbled to the floor. Tears blurred her eyes, and she blinked.

Lester's face was peaceful as though he'd gone to sleep, as though everything was all right now.

Determined to be quiet because of Tom, she closed the door and rested her back against it.

Death had always been a part of life for her. Her parents had died when she was just five years old. She'd always been fascinated by it.

By what came after.

She'd tried strangling a cat once as a child.

Its incessant meowing had disrupted her studying. She'd later found out the cat had been ill and in pain, but while she'd been in the middle of preparing for an important exam, she'd felt nothing but hate for the animal.

She'd poured her frustrations into her grip.

Her grandmother's cruelty. Her older brother's indifference.

Her parents' death.

Her first boyfriend's rejection and mocking of her after she'd asked him to the school dance.

She'd wrapped her hands around the cat's neck, and she'd squeezed.

Its eyes had bulged with terror.

"Stop interrupting me," she'd hissed through gritted teeth. She still remembered the way she'd flinched upon realising that she hadn't recognised her own voice.

She'd let go and dropped the cat.

It had run off, but she'd never forget the look on its face.

So unlike the look on Lester's face right now.

She'd been thirteen at the time. Tom's age.

She'd felt that urge over and over again. The urge to squeeze the life out of people.

Not regularly, but enough times to have had to step out of patients' rooms occasionally.

She'd never harm a person, of course, but she'd always wondered if other people felt this urge.

Had Tom ever felt it?

She blinked. Were Lester's eyelids fluttering?

No. It had to be her imagination. There was too much blood for him to be alive. The coppery smell of it had filled the room. Pungent and sweet.

Chris swallowed.

She crawled to the bed on all fours. She'd told him to kill himself. She'd told him they'd be better off without him.

She'd done this.

This was on her.

His grey lips formed a small *o* as if forever accusing her of what she'd done.

Of what she'd said.

She pressed two fingers against the side of his neck. No pulse. Lester—the man who'd always forgiven her—had finally stopped forgiving.

And Tom was down the hallway. In his room. Unaware.

Grey dots danced across her vision, her ears ringing.

Could she get Lester's body out of the house? Without Tom knowing?

She'd moved to Harlow from Waltham Abbey to be closer to the hospital for work. She had no family in Harlow. No friends. Nowhere to go.

She'd cut off all contact with her grandmother and her brother a long time ago, and her shifts hadn't permitted her to find close friends.

The only person she knew in Harlow was Anna.

Chris placed her hands against the windowsill and steadied herself.

What was she going to do?

It had taken the government a few days to mobilise the army. With only makeshift communications in place, it must have been difficult to deploy the soldiers in an organised manner.

But they were here now. Patrolling the streets.

Guarding the supermarkets.

Dropping off care packages.

She frowned, pulling up her inventory in her mind and doing some calculations. With Lester gone, Chris and her son could survive for three months.

And if she was able to plant tomatoes and potatoes…

But what about Lester's body? His parents had died a few years ago, and he'd been an only child.

What was she supposed to do? Hand him over to the army? Would they investigate his death? Would they find out about Mike?

Would they think she was to blame and arrest her?

She considered burying Lester in her garden. Perhaps while Tom was sleeping.

But what would she say to her son?

What if Tom found out what she'd said to Lester?

If she left with Tom, how long would it take for someone to find the body?

A loud knock on the door made her flinch.

Tom.

"Mum?"

She took a deep breath, hoping her voice wouldn't shake. "I'll be right outside, sweetie."

He'd never forgive her if he found out that she was responsible for his father's death, if he found out what she'd said.

Chris braced herself, opened the door and slipped out into the hallway.

7

Fear had taken over her entire body, leaving her breathless. She gritted her teeth to stop them from chattering as her whole body shook. The reality of Lester's death was sinking in, overwhelming her.

What had tipped him over the edge?

You.

Facing her son, Chris took a deep breath. "I think we should leave. Find a place that's easier to defend."

"Mum? What's the matter? You look pale."

"I'm fine, sweetie."

"Where's Dad?"

Chris hid a trembling hand behind her back. "He's still sleeping."

"Now? It's almost dinnertime." Tom frowned. "What's going on? Mum?"

Her thoughts whirled through her mind like a tornado. Tom wouldn't believe her if she told him that Lester had left. Fled. Abandoned them.

Perhaps if she set the house on fire—*don't be ridiculous.* As if the air had been knocked out of her, Chris deflated and her shoulders slumped. Tears spilled down her cheeks. "Don't go in there, Tom. It's not how you want to remember him."

Tom placed his hand on the doorknob and looked at her, his eyes widening as the truth dawned on him.

He'd feared this would happen, and she'd assured him it wouldn't. *Your dad will get better.* An empty promise—turned to dust in a single day.

She watched helplessly as he took a deep breath and braced himself for what he was about to see.

"Don't go in there, Tom," Chris pleaded.

He'd never forgive her. He'd abandon her like everyone else.

"I have to." Tom opened the door, stepped inside, and Chris heard him gasp. Her heart broke at the sound.

She followed her son, stifling a sob with her hand.

With the blinds closed, the bedroom was gloomy. Chris rubbed her eyes. It had been so bright earlier, the blood a glaring red.

She didn't remember closing the blinds.

"You said he wouldn't do this," Tom whispered, and this time his voice was filled with as much accusation as a thirteen-year-old could possibly muster.

Chris stared at her dead husband's face as her son wept.

She thought back to the night they'd met. Lester had sat near the bar, tapping away on his laptop, pale blue eyes huge behind thick round glasses, his curly hair in need of a comb or—better yet—a cut.

She overheard him ordering a beer, blushing and shy. When the waitress brought it over, she dropped it, spilling the contents of the glass all over his trousers and laptop.

He didn't even flinch. Said no harsh words. Instead, he quickly moved his laptop and books to a dry spot and helped the waitress clean up the mess.

"Gosh! Is your computer dead?" the waitress asked, soaking up the beer with a cloth. Tears laced her words.

Lester smiled. "It's fine. Don't worry about it."

Chris turned her head slightly in his direction, listening to the conversation instead of paying attention to her fellow nursing students. She didn't believe for a moment that his keyboard had survived.

Minutes later, the owner of the bar himself brought over a new beer, apologising profusely, and offering to replace the laptop.

Lester politely declined, wiping his stained trousers with a napkin. His nostrils flared as he smelled himself, the unmistakable odour of beer now his cologne for the night. He stayed for a while longer, sipping his new beer and scribbling into a leather-bound notebook.

Chris asked him out before he left. She wasn't prepared to let a man like him walk away. Someone who didn't get angry.

Someone who would put up with her and love her—unlike her brother and grandmother who'd spent the twenty years prior telling her that nobody would ever want to be with her unless they were forced to.

Lester. Sweet and patient Lester, who was kind when Chris was unkind, patient when Chris got agitated, and supportive when Chris needed support the most.

He gave her a family. Promised to stick with her no matter what she did.

And now he was gone.

Because of her.

Because she'd told him to. Her brother and grandmother had been right, after all. Nobody wanted to be with her. Nobody wanted to put up with her.

Nobody wanted her.

"We need to leave," Chris said, placing a hand on Tom's arm.

He flinched and jerked his arm away. "Mum…" His voice was quiet, soft. His hands trembled.

"What is it?"

"Why…why are you covered in blood?"

"Wha—" She looked down and froze. Her skin was caked with dried blood all the way up to her elbows where it had seeped into her shirt, staining it an angry red.

The crust on her white sleeves looked like rust on metal.

"Mum? Did you hurt Dad?"

Shocked, she stared at her son. "No. Why would you…" She swallowed. "We were talking in your room just now, and then I came in here…and I found him…"

"Mum, *we* were talking in my room this morning. You said you'd go and get some sleep hours ago. It's late afternoon."

Sobs choked her, and she turned to look outside. Through the blinds she caught a glimpse of the sun, a bright orange above the horizon.

"Mum…I saw what you did to your…to Mike."

"No, honey, this isn't—" She dropped to her knees and stared at her hands.

She *was* responsible for Lester's death. At least her words were. She didn't…she hadn't…

Chris closed her eyes, unable to face the grief on her son's face.

She'd experienced a blackout *once*, had only been sixteen years old at the time.

She'd been dating her first boyfriend for two months when he'd told her he was seeing someone else. She'd wept, pleaded, begged, then screamed, and he'd thrown her out of the house.

The police had found her in the early hours of the following morning, wandering through the woods behind

Carl's house. She hadn't known where she'd been, hadn't known what she'd done since she'd left.

She'd insisted no more than an hour had passed at the most, but it had been almost twelve.

Her brother, Stuart, had admitted her to the hospital, insisted they call a psychiatrist, but they'd sent her home saying she was neither a danger to herself nor to others. "Stress can cause such an episode," a doctor had said to Stuart. "She needs to sleep more."

That would explain everything, Chris thought. Just like back then, she hadn't slept, had spent the night working. She must have fallen asleep or passed out from shock.

"Mum?"

Tom's voice interrupted her thoughts.

"It must have happened while I checked his pulse. I must have touched..." She grabbed a towel from the chest of drawers by the door and scrubbed her hands.

Grief cut through her chest like a knife. Lester's coagulated blood clung to her skin like glue and her son watched her with wide eyes as if she were a monster and not his mother. "I'm sorry you had to see this."

Tom sniffled and wiped his nose. "Mum? Did you hurt Dad?" he asked again, and she shook her head.

"No. No. I swear. I didn't."

"But..."

"We have to leave, Tom. We can't stay here."

"Where would we go? Uncle Stuart's?" He backed away from the bed, from his dad, and pressed his back against the wall. Sliding to the floor, he buried his face in his hands.

"No. Not Uncle Stuart." If she never saw her older brother again it would be too soon. "No. We're going to a friend of mine. Anna. She lives near the hospital."

Tom didn't look up. "The soldiers won't allow us to leave the house."

"I have my NHS badge. It's easier for me to get to work from Anna's. They'll understand."

Don't ever hesitate, Chris. Act. Those had been Anna's words. And everything she'd said so far had turned out to be true.

"I'm scared," Tom whispered.

"I know, sweetie." Chris dropped the towel and reached out to hug Tom, but he backed away.

"What about dad? We can't just leave him here. We need to tell someone."

"We can't go to the police. Not after what happened with Mike. They'll think I did this. They'll take you away."

"You're scaring me, Mum."

Chris pinched the bridge of her nose. She had to think. Fast. "Once people realise the government is letting them starve, they'll riot, and once the soldiers out there understand that the government isn't helping their families either, they'll abandon their posts." She paused, took a deep breath. "Your dad wouldn't want for us to be separated. Believe me, Tom."

"Did he leave a note? Anything?" Tom crawled to his feet. He rummaged through Lester's wardrobe and drawers, then left the room. Moments later, she heard him search Lester's office.

Chris studied Lester's body. The slashed wrists. The blood.

She searched his face for answers.

It had been early in the morning when she'd left Tom's bedroom.

She didn't remember anything that happened after that. Until she'd found the body.

Had she done this?

She stared at her palms. How had she lost an entire day?

"Is it even safe to go outside?" Tom asked from the hallway.

Chris left the bedroom and closed the door behind her. "For now, yes, but not for long. People feel safe in numbers, but currently they're confined to their homes, isolated. It'll be a few more days before all hell breaks loose."

A family portrait hung on the wall near the stairs. Silent accusations filled Lester's eyes as he stared at her from the photo.

Don't be silly.

Tom squared his jaw. "Everyone should just leave their homes at the same time. What could the army do about it?"

"Shoot people. At least the first few." Chris raised an eyebrow. "Are you willing to be the first? Are you willing to sacrifice yourself?"

Tom shrugged. His spindly arms hung limply at his side. Grief had hardened his eyes. "Who is Anna? You've never mentioned her before."

"A friend. You'll like her." Chris smiled. "I promise." She didn't know if the woman she'd randomly met at Tesco would even be open to Chris and Tom joining her.

If they brought enough supplies…perhaps.

"She lives in a flat on the top floor. Easier to defend than a house."

With Lester dead, they couldn't stay here.

Anna would understand.

"Should we bury Dad before we go?"

Chris barely recognised her son's face as he pulled his mouth into an ugly grimace. "I'm not sure how to dig a grave without our next-door neighbours seeing."

Tom scowled.

"We'll come back for him. Once we're safe and sorted." It was an empty promise, but Tom was thirteen, and she didn't know what else to say.

"I don't believe you," he said quietly. "And I'm not sure I believe you didn't kill him."

"Why would I—" She stopped, stared at her son's face, searching his eyes for a sign of compassion. "I'm sorry, Tom. I haven't been there for your dad. I've messed up. I know that. But I'd never hurt him. I'd never do this."

He bit down on his bottom lip, staring at the closed bedroom door. "If you say so."

Chris held her tongue as she decided not to reply. She poured her frustration and sadness into filling a suitcase with supplies, covering them with clothes. She asked Tom to do the same.

She put on her NHS uniform and badge and attached the bright orange band to her arm before leaving the house. Her heart pounded in her chest as she set foot onto the street.

They would see it on her face.

Lester's death.

Her guilt.

A soldier immediately approached her, one hand on the barrel of the assault rifle strapped to his chest. "Madam, you're not allowed—" Noticing her badge, he gave her a curt nod. "You're allowed to go to work, of course." He forced a smile. "But why are you taking the boy and the suitcases?"

Chris wrung her hands, hoping her voice wouldn't betray her. "I work at the hospital, but I don't feel safe on my way there. It's a forty-minute walk and I worry." A sheepish smile appeared on her lips. "Someone might overlook my badge and…" She gave his rifle a pointed look.

The soldier narrowed his eyes but waited for her to continue.

"I have a friend who lives on Fifth Avenue, near Sainsbury's. She has enough space for me and my son, and I'd be five minutes away from work." She hoped he wouldn't ask for the exact address.

"Does your friend know you're coming?"

Chris bit back a sarcastic comment. It wouldn't help. It

never did. Instead she sighed. "Unfortunately, I don't have any way of informing her ahead of time."

"I'll organise an escort," the soldier said. "I don't want you walking down the street with suitcases. People might see and…I'll send for a car."

"You have working cars?"

"We've—" He stopped as though remembering that she was a civilian.

"Do you know what happened?" Chris asked.

"That's classified."

Behind her, Tom craned his neck. "Was it a solar flare?"

The soldier didn't even acknowledge Tom's presence and instead said to Chris, "Please remain in your home until I can get a car to you."

He turned, took two steps, then looked back at her. "What's in the suitcases?"

Chris felt the blood drain from her face. "Clothes, work uniforms, work shoes, tinned food. I doubt my friend was planning on feeding two more people, so I figured I'd pack what I have." She offered a small, timid smile, hoping the soldier wouldn't notice her shaking hands.

He gave her a long look, and she forced herself to meet his eyes. Her heart hammered against her ribcage. Any moment now, he'd open her suitcases and find their food.

Find her pepper spray. Her knives.

She clenched and unclenched her fists. Held her breath. Waited.

Finally, the soldier's face relaxed, and his lips curled into a smile. "I'll knock when we're ready."

8

Anna's flat was less than ten minutes away by car, the lack of traffic making the journey even quicker. Chris sat with her shoulders tense the entire way, digging her nails into her palms until she drew blood.

What if Anna didn't let her in? What if Anna told the driver that she'd never seen Chris before, and the driver took her back to her house, where Lester was?

The seats of the doorless Jeep were uncomfortable, and the wind blew strands of her hair into her face. Dark grey clouds threatened rain.

Tom pressed himself into a corner of the vehicle, holding his bag in a white-knuckled grip. He didn't meet her eyes.

"It's so empty. Spooky," he mumbled as they drove past the buildings surrounding the town centre, turning right towards Sainsbury's.

A roadblock manned by several soldiers stopped anyone from entering the town centre.

Pillars of smoke rose above Terminus House. Chris craned her neck in search of the fire as they turned the corner but couldn't see anything out of the ordinary.

Was the army beginning to lose control?

Was the smoke a sign of riots?

Moments later, Chris gestured for the driver to stop. "This is it. Wait here," she said to Tom, jumping out of the Jeep.

She ran up to the front door and rang the bell before realising that wouldn't work. Stepping away from the building, she tilted her head back and shouted Anna's name. A raindrop hit her face, rolling down her cheek. She brought up her arm to protect her face when a window opened, then slammed shut again.

A few minutes later, the front door opened a crack and Anna stuck her head out, frowning. "Chris?" Spotting the army vehicle in the street, she narrowed her eyes. "What are you doing here?"

Behind her stood a small black and white Border Collie. His ears lay flat against the sides of his head, his lips pulled up, revealing sharp teeth bared in a silent snarl. The hair on the back of his neck stood on end.

Chris didn't hesitate and, with a wide grin, pulled Anna into a hug, whispering, "I need your help. Pretend that we're good friends. I'll explain later."

Anna stiffened.

"Please," Chris repeated. Feeling Anna squeeze the small of her back, Chris slumped into the hug. Relief washed over her. "Thank you," she said through tears.

She turned and waved for Tom to get out of the Jeep. "Bring the suitcases."

The soldier gave her a curt nod and helped Tom with the luggage before driving off without a backward glance.

"This is Tom," Chris said, and Anna stuck out her hand. Tom shook it reluctantly. His eyes were bloodshot, his face pale.

The Border Collie was barking now, his bushy tail pointed at the sky. "This is Oreo. He's not a fan of strangers." Anna looked down at her dog and placed her index finger against her lips. "Hush. These are friends." Oreo whined in response.

She turned her attention to the two suitcases Tom had dragged to the front door and lifted an eyebrow in question.

"I'll explain later," Chris said and pointed at the suitcases. "I've brought supplies." She didn't want Anna to think she was expecting anything more than a place to stay. "It's enough to feed us for a while. I don't expect anything from you. Just…a safe place…if at all possible?"

Anna didn't reply, instead opened the door wide in invitation. The expression on her face was unreadable. Chris couldn't tell whether she was pleased to have company or if they had intruded on her peace.

Now that she got a look at Anna in daylight, she realised the woman was almost forty. She wore her dark blonde hair short. Her face was long and angular, her jaw and chin pointy, giving her the look of someone who didn't put up with anyone's nonsense.

Chris wondered why Anna lived alone and if she had any children.

And if not, why?

"I'd love to offer you tea," Anna said heading up the stairs. "But interestingly enough, my kettle doesn't work." Arriving at the top of the stairs, Anna opened the door to her flat and waited for Oreo to slip inside. "Where is your hu—"

"I'll tell you later." Chris' eyes flicked to Tom, but he was still at the bottom of the stairs, awkwardly struggling with his suitcase, banging the wheels against every other step.

"How come that Jeep was still working?" Anna asked. "And how come they let you out? I thought we weren't supposed to leave the house."

Chris took off her lanyard and showed Anna the badge. "I work for the NHS. As for the vehicle…I'm not sure. Tom?"

Tom shrugged, dumping Chris' suitcase by the door. "I

don't know. Perhaps it's just that old? I'll get your case, Mum." Before Chris could reply he ran back down the stairs.

"And you're staying here?" Anna asked.

"If that's all right with you?" Chris held one hand up to her face to muffle her voice. "My husband's dead."

Anna's eyes widened.

At that moment, Tom reached the top of the stairs, panting, his face flushed and sweaty. "How much stuff did you bring?"

"Well, this is a two-bedroom flat," Anna said. "There isn't much space, but if you don't mind sleeping in the same room, there's a sofa in the spare room which converts into a rather comfortable bed." Anna closed the front door behind them and locked it. "I mostly use the spare room for storage and to hang my washing. I'm afraid it's a bit messy.

"Don't worry," Chris said.

It was getting late. The light was fading.

"I'm going to bed," Tom announced.

"Don't you want—"

"I'm going to bed."

He hadn't said more than a few words to her since they'd left their home. Tears stung her eyes as she watched him shuffle down the hallway. "Here?" he asked, and Anna nodded.

"Shout if you need anything," Chris said, but he didn't reply and instead slammed the door closed behind him.

Anna pointed at another door. "Living room is through there. Make yourself at home. I found half an empty bottle of whisky stashed behind some olive oil and soy sauce earlier today if you fancy a drink?"

Chris sank into the sofa cushions and rubbed her eyes. Whisky sounded just like what she needed. "Thank you."

Oreo was sitting on a dog bed next to the sofa licking his paws.

"Can I pet him?" Chris asked.

"He'll come to you once he feels comfortable." Anna walked into the room, holding the bottle of whisky in one hand and two glasses in the other. "I rarely drink." She handed Chris one of the glasses. "And I can't offer any ice for obvious reasons."

"At least whisky doesn't go off." Chris lifted her glass and smiled. "Thank you, Anna." She took a sip, savouring the smooth drink warming her insides.

"Tell me about your husband," Anna said, sitting down on the sofa. She flicked a match and lit the three candles on the coffee table.

Oreo looked up from his bed and tilted his head, his black eyes watching Chris.

Chris snorted. "Where do I start?"

"Where is he?"

"Back home."

Anna clasped her hand over her mouth. "You just…left him there?"

"What was I supposed to do?" Chris shifted.

"Are you and Tom okay?"

Chris sobbed. "I'm to blame." The words escaped her mouth before she could stop them. She didn't know this woman, didn't know if she could trust her, but she couldn't keep it together.

"What do you mean?"

"I—" Chris hesitated, rubbing the nape of her neck. "The night I met you…after I got home…" She stared into her drink, swirling the golden liquid around in her glass. "Tom had left to find me in the middle of the night, and I was so angry at Lester for not stopping him. I told him…I told him we'd be better off without him."

Anna didn't say anything, silently sipping her whisky.

Chris didn't know where to start. How much to reveal. After all, she didn't want the other woman to throw her out.

Nobody will ever love you, Chris. It should have been you. Not Mum and Dad. You.

Stuart's voice. Chris squeezed her eyes shut. "My family life is…such a mess." She laughed.

Anna smiled. "Isn't everyone's?"

Chris began to talk. She told Anna about Lester's depression. How he'd struggled to get out of bed, do the little things. How his job performance had deteriorated, and how she'd had to take on a second job to make ends meet. She talked about Tom, about how much teenagers ate, and how her salary hadn't been enough to pay the bills and the mortgage.

A mortgage they'd taken out based on Lester's salary.

"What about insurance?" Anna asked.

"We only took out critical illness insurance. We'd prepared for cancer or a stroke. They don't cover depression. I love my job at the hospital, but it just doesn't pay enough." Chris took another sip of her drink. "It should have been me, you know. I should have been the one afflicted with something as awful as depression because Lester would have been able to deal with me. He was kind and supportive and patient."

The words tumbled freely from her mouth. Chris didn't stop to think, didn't filter, just spoke.

"I have no doubt that he'd have lifted me up and carried me through." She sighed. "But it was him. He was the one who suffered, and I'm not patient, and I wasn't able to help him. When he told me that Tom had left the house to find me in the middle of the night after the…after what happened, I felt so angry. I told him that I wished he'd kill himself. And he did." She chuckled dryly. "And he did."

Anna remained silent, leaning her head back against the sofa cushions.

"Tom saw him. If he ever finds out what I said…if he finds out that I'm the reason his father is dead, he'll never speak to me again."

Anna took a sip of her whisky. Her flushed cheeks appeared bright red in the candlelight. She hadn't been lying when she'd said she didn't drink much. "I haven't listened to my dad's last voicemail. He called me the day it happened. I never got the chance to listen."

Chris furrowed her brows. Where was Anna going with this? If her worst crime was not to have listened to her father's voicemail, she must have led a very sheltered life.

"He's diabetic. Without insulin, he'll die soon. Or perhaps…" Anna shrugged. "That stuff needs refrigerating, doesn't it?"

Chris nodded.

"He has one of those automatic dispensers. I don't even know if he still has the equipment to administer insulin without it."

"Insulin can be kept at room temperature for a few weeks. I could get you some from the hospital. Does he live nearby? We could check in on him if you'd like." Chris smiled. "Tom said something about perhaps finding working electronics. Perhaps we could look for a small fridge?"

"Even if we find one, we can't plug it in, can we?"

"We'd also need a generator."

Chris watched as Anna chewed on the inside of her cheek. A shadow crept into her eyes. Guilt? Anger?

"What happens once we run out of insulin? Or fuel to run the generator?"

"One day at a time, right? You can't just give up on your father. This whole EMP thing…perhaps they'll fix it. It might only be temporary. You never know."

Anna took a deep breath. "I didn't listen to my father's last voicemail because his voice makes my blood run cold. He's a violent drunk." She wrinkled her nose. "When my mum died of cancer twelve years ago, he insisted on a third of the ashes. My sister and I got the other two thirds. I can't believe Mum refused to leave him." Anna scoffed. "Said she'd made a promise to God. And he...he flushed his third down the toilet. He filmed himself doing it and sent us the video. Said she had it coming."

Chris swallowed. "Or..." she said quietly, "I won't bring back any insulin from the hospital."

"I vote you don't." Anna giggled. It was obviously an involuntary sound, and she pressed her palm against her mouth to suppress the hysterical laughter bubbling up. "Does that make me a horrible person?"

"No." Chris considered telling Anna about killing Mike and how it had made her feel. Tall. Powerful. Important. As if for one single moment the fate of the universe lay in her hands and she was in charge of both life and death.

At that moment, she'd felt like she could do anything.

Face anyone.

She thought of Tom's reaction to seeing her covered in blood and how he'd looked at her as if she was a monster and not his mother. He thought she'd hurt Lester.

Had she? Was that even possible?

She'd lost hours, almost an entire day.

Chris opened her mouth, then closed it again. Anna wouldn't understand.

Letting an estranged father die was different to murdering her boss, even if he had threatened her son.

"You mentioned you had a sister? Sarah?" Chris said instead. "Where does she live?"

"Colchester."

"Married? Children?"

Anna laughed. "Not yet, but she's only thirty-two."

"Do you know where she is?"

"No. Are we the odd ones out for not having come up with a plan for emergencies? Is everybody else prepared?" Anna tilted her head back and emptied her glass.

"I doubt it," Chris said. "Lester and I didn't even have wills prepared and we have a son. I wouldn't know how to get back home if you dropped me five miles from here. Not without a sat nav. Do you think she'll be coming to Harlow?"

Anna shrugged. "We joked about it one evening over a glass of wine. She said she'd come here, but I'm pretty sure she meant by car."

"Are you going to look for her?"

"Maybe? But what if she shows up while I'm gone? What if we're doomed to eternally miss each other and wander around Essex?" Anna reached for the bottle. "More whisky?"

Chris held out her empty glass for a refill. "Thank you."

Anna stood and poured them both another drink. "How much food did you bring?"

"I brought enough for three months. Maybe four. Ideally, I'd like to have enough for six months. Have you signed up to the food supply scheme?"

"I tried to, but I was worried they might search houses to make sure nobody took more than they needed. What if they found the food I've already stashed away?"

Chris traced the edge of her glass with a finger. "You're right. That's a risk."

"Besides, the government will run out of food within a month. There is no way they have enough to feed the entire population for long. Aren't we pretty much dependent on imports these days?"

"I'm not sure," Chris said.

"The city centre is blocked off by the army. Any unguarded supermarket has to be empty."

"What about the Poundland warehouse?" Chris asked.

"I'm guessing that will either be empty or guarded too. Why? What are you thinking?"

"I could try and sneak in…pretend somebody needs medical help. I could take Tom. Attempt a distraction."

"And get shot?"

Chris laughed. "There's that risk, of course."

"Can't we just stay here? Wait it out?"

"I don't know. I don't know how long it'll take for the riots to subside. Right now, the people still believe it'll all go back to normal. Once they start fighting over scraps, it'll be impossible to find food. What if we run out of food and…it's not over?" She sat up. "I need something to eat."

"I have—"

"No, don't worry. Relax." Chris found her suitcase in the hallway and opened it. Retrieving a Tupperware container, she glanced at the door to Anna's spare room.

Tom. He no longer trusted her. What was she going to do? How was she going to keep him safe?

"Are you all right?" Anna asked.

Chris took the container with her into the living room and removed the lid, offering the contents to Anna. "Homemade peanut butter oatmeal honey bars. Want one?"

Anna shook her head. "No, thank you."

"The ideal fuel for an apocalypse, and there's no need to bake them."

Anna frowned, staring past Chris at her open suitcase.

"What?"

"Is that rat poison?"

Chris shrugged. "I thought it might come in useful. I hate rats, but they'll probably thrive. Lots of bodies to feast on. Lots of empty houses. And later when we want to grow food—"

"Ewww." Anna grimaced. She put her glass down and

drew the curtains before leaning back into the cushions. "It's been what…seven days? If Sarah had tried to walk to Harlow from Colchester, she'd have been here by now."

"How far away is Colchester?"

"Forty miles?"

"That's a long walk."

"I know."

"But?"

"I have to find her. I promised Mum I'd take care of her. How many working vehicles do you think the army has?"

"I can't imagine they have many. They only helped me because they're trying to keep the hospital going. I saw quite a few injured soldiers during my shift last night."

"When's your next shift?"

"Tomorrow night." Chris yawned. "Tom and I can look after the flat for you if you want to find your sister. Come straight back. It's not safe out there."

Anna sighed. "What about Oreo?"

"Is he a good guard dog?" Chris asked. "Can he protect you?"

"Inside? Yes. He'll bark whenever someone comes up the stairs. Outside? Not so much. He's more likely to bark and hide than bite."

"In that case leave him here where he can help protect our supplies."

"What do we do in a few months?" Anna asked.

"What do you mean?"

"You said you're worried that we'll run out of food before it's over."

"I am. I don't want to have to find food in the middle of a civil war." Her head felt heavy, and Chris closed her eyes. "If they can't fix the grid, we'll have to find a place to grow food, but I'd feel much calmer knowing that won't be necessary for the next few months."

"Perhaps trying to get into the Poundland warehouse is worth a thought after all?"

"You find your sister, and I find us some more food?"

Anna smiled. "And when this is all over, we'll have to find chickens, a cow, a goat…we could learn how to hunt."

Chris opened one eye. "And then what? Find a community of like-minded people who are willing to live together and work together?"

"Exactly."

"You're not joking? And what if nobody takes in strangers by that point?"

"I don't know, but where would we go *now*?" Anna asked. "Soldiers are patrolling the streets. I don't know anyone who owns a farm. We can't just go knocking on people's doors. No. We have to wait until the worst is over."

"Until most people have died, you mean."

Anna met her eyes. "Yes." She shrugged and giggled before taking another sip. "Until we're the only ones left."

Chris raised her glass in a toast. "Until we're the only ones left."

9

ANNA HADN'T SLEPT A WINK BEFORE SETTING OUT IN THE early hours of the morning.

She yawned, pushing thorny branches to the side as she fought her way through the brambles growing along the side of the road. Her legs felt heavy, her calves tight, threatening to cramp.

She'd never walked more than ten miles before, let alone forty, and had no idea how long it would take her to reach Colchester. Could she do it in two days?

Tendrils of black smoke rose over Stansted. Although it had been close to midnight when the EMP had hit, it wasn't impossible that a plane had crashed.

The pungent smell of smoke seemed to accompany her wherever she went. She'd first smelled it in Harlow, faint but distinct. Out here, it grew stronger.

It had been an exceptionally dry June. Without electricity, people had to rely on candles for light and on open fires to cook.

Without engines and water pumps, firefighters couldn't do their jobs.

It was a recipe for disaster.

Anna crouched down, massaging first her left then her right calf. Running two miles every other day hadn't prepared her for this.

Not in the slightest.

The road was deserted save for the odd, abandoned car, but Anna felt safer hidden behind the adjacent thicket. She patted her trouser pocket to make sure the can of pepper spray was still there.

Chris had handed it to her the night before. "You never know," she'd said. "It might be useful."

How long would the army keep people inside?

How much longer would peace last?

A warm drizzle fell, seeping into her clothes. Retrieving a jacket from her backpack, she yawned again, and a shiver ran down her spine. She'd forgotten to put out a bucket to collect rainwater. Hopefully, Chris would remember.

Pulling her hood up, she continued her hike.

Sleep had eluded her. Tossing and turning in her bed, she'd spent the whole night worrying. Worrying about the strangers in her flat, about leaving Oreo behind and about the long trek to Colchester.

Could she trust Chris? A stranger?

Chris was a nurse. Someone with medical knowledge. Someone who would know which antibiotics to take if Anna happened to come down with pneumonia come winter. That was useful.

She'd even offered to bring back insulin for Anna's father.

He lived only minutes away from Harlow. Despite having left home at a young age, Anna had never managed to get out of the town she'd been born and raised in.

He was family. They shared blood.

What if Sarah had gone there?

No. Sarah would go to Harlow first.

Anna shook her head and groaned. Squeezing her eyes shut, she rubbed her aching forehead, thankful for the thick clouds shielding her from the summer sun. She was too old to drink more than two glasses of whisky.

Through the bushes, she spotted something on the road and narrowed her eyes, pulling a branch to the side for a better look.

Just a motorbike.

Where *was* Sarah? When the army vehicle had pulled up outside her flat, Anna had hoped to see Sarah. It would have been just like her sister to convince a soldier to drive her across Essex—but no, it had been Chris. Even if her sister had only walked five to seven miles a day, she *should* have been in Harlow by now.

Images of her sister dead in a ditch, or lying somewhere and slowly bleeding out, flashed through Anna's mind and she winced.

She'd never forgive herself if her sister was hurt.

She'd promised her mum she'd look after Sarah. She'd *promised*.

As children, they hadn't liked each other. Their father had adored Sarah and abhorred Anna. As the golden child, Sarah had been showered with praise. He'd fulfilled her every wish.

Their mum had brought them together, taught them to love each other and look after each other.

But Anna had fled and left her childhood home as soon as she had been able to.

Anna sniffed, her thoughts drifting back to Oreo and the way he'd sat by the door when she left, hanging his head, whining softly. He'd been her companion for years. He had always made her feel safe, and he'd even driven away the occasional, awkward late-night flirting attempt with his bark.

But if she had to hide from someone and keep quiet?

Just like most Border Collies, Oreo was vocal whenever

he felt anxious or threatened, and considering the way the world had changed overnight, his nervous bark would likely have given her away at the wrong moment.

And while Chris was indeed a stranger, she had a son to protect, and Oreo *was* the perfect guard for the flat. He'd never missed anyone coming up the stairs. Always barked.

Unless it was Sarah.

Whenever Sarah visited, he'd wag his tail, spinning around by the door.

Oreo would help Chris look after her son, and he'd wait for Anna to come back.

Not that Chris needed any help.

She'd left a dead husband at home, grabbed her teenage son and somehow convinced a soldier to drive her from one end of Harlow to the other.

Anna wondered what she would have done, had she been in Chris' shoes. *Probably not told my husband that I wished he'd kill himself.* Anna snorted.

She'd seen a hardness in Chris' eyes, and the deep lines around her mouth gave Chris the appearance of someone who was eternally bitter. The timid smile she'd flashed Anna every now and then was almost certainly for show, and the way she pursed her lips as if sucking lemons fuelled that suspicion.

That didn't *necessarily* mean she couldn't be trusted.

Anna hadn't mentioned the food packets hidden in her wardrobe, not wanting to reveal everything about herself just yet, but—how far would a mother go to protect her son?

Anna's longest relationship had lasted six years before they'd broken up because she hadn't wanted children. He had. They'd both known from the very first date, but they'd both thought they'd change each other's minds.

Alas, they hadn't been able to.

They'd broken up five years ago. Anna had lived alone

ever since. Other people made her uncomfortable. She preferred Oreo and her shelves filled with books.

A thought entered her mind. Did she owe it to her father to check in on him?

Did she owe anything to someone who had made her childhood miserable? Who'd been nothing but abusive? Did she owe the man who'd flushed her mum's ashes down the toilet any courtesy?

Chris had offered to get some insulin from the hospital.

No.

Anna came to a halt under a tree that shielded her from the rain and pulled out the map she'd found in her loft along with her camping gear. She traced the roads with her index finger, squinting as she rotated the map.

Which way was north again?

She'd hoped to walk the forty miles in two days. Studying her progress on the map, she snorted. Blisters were forming on her heels, and she'd walked, at most, eight miles.

When the first rays of sunlight had drifted in through her window, Anna had said goodbye to Oreo and slipped outside, avoiding the soldiers patrolling the road in front of her house. She'd crept along side streets, keeping close to buildings.

She'd stopped for the first time by the river an hour later. Rested for a moment.

Sarah should have been in Harlow by now.

Anna couldn't shake the feeling that something awful had happened.

Or she went to check on Dad.

Again, that nagging thought. A pang of guilt made her wince.

"You don't owe him anything," she muttered, glancing up at the sky. The rain was growing heavier, fat drops rolling off her jacket. Wiping the sweat from her brow, she scowled. "You don't owe him anything."

Anna had never believed that and always struggled with the feelings her father evoked in her.

She sighed and shook her head.

Sarah first. She'd deal with her father later.

She'd have to sleep outside, find shelter somewhere halfway. Away from housing. Away from the road. Ten miles to go until she could rest.

At least it wasn't cold.

EVERY BONE in her body ached when she woke up the next morning. Sitting up, she massaged her shoulders, slowly stretching her neck until the tendons popped.

She'd stumbled upon the bench by nightfall, too exhausted to eat, and had simply curled up in her sleeping bag.

She pulled out her map. Twenty-five miles to go before she'd reach Colchester. The previous day she'd followed the route of the A120 and had kept close to the road. It circled Braintree, but Anna worried there might be police or soldiers patrolling the exits.

She didn't want to risk being spotted and taken into custody for ignoring the curfew.

Not after what had happened to her neighbour.

Anna buttoned her jacket and shouldered her bag. The rain had stopped at some point during the night, and the occasional gap in the grey clouds allowed the sun to peek through.

She walked along a field, away from the road, searching for a footpath. Her heels burned where the blisters had popped.

A dull ache spread from her knee to her hip. Every step hurt. When had she got so old?

Wet fabric stuck to her skin and she shivered. Her nail

beds had turned blue. Her trousers were chafing the skin of her thighs. If only she'd brought a change of clothes.

She hummed a song to distract herself.

Once she passed Braintree, she could get back onto the road and follow it straight to Colchester. She could do this. She had to.

She'd find Sarah and—

Her foot hit something soft, and she stumbled. She caught herself and a jolt of pain surged through her knee. "What the —" She looked down. A sob escaped her lips, and she pressed her palm against her mouth.

A woman was lying in the tall grass. Blood had seeped from a hole in her forehead down her temple and into her brown hair. Her eyes were staring up at the sky, wide open and lifeless.

There was another body next to her, his arm draped across her waist. He'd been shot through the chest. The blood had dried on his shirt.

At his feet lay a third body. Another woman. She was lying on her stomach, her blonde hair crusted with blood. A chunk of flesh was missing from her thigh, exposing white bone.

Flies buzzed, settling on the bodies.

Anna sobbed, her shoulders shaking. She turned, searching the field. Behind her, near a small patch of woodland, she spotted a farmhouse. The fence ran along the edge of the field.

A curtain twitched. A dog barked.

Anna ran towards the road, away from the farmhouse.

Being allowed to protect their livestock meant that farmers often owned guns. Was that what had happened here? Farmers protecting their property?

Would this be the new normal? Bodies littering the streets and fields? People defending their homes?

Anna hoisted herself over the fence and onto the road where she stopped, panting. She placed her hands on her thighs, waiting for her breathing to slow.

Had the army already lost control in parts of the country? How many people owned guns? How many were prepared to kill to protect their families?

Was the prime minister still in charge?

Was there still a government? How many people would patiently wait for them to introduce food rations, only to realise that there was nothing to ration.

Where would we go? she'd asked Chris the night before. Anyone who had a safe place to offer would defend it, just like that farmer had defended his land.

She pulled out her map. Perhaps walking along the road—

"Hello," a voice said.

Anna dropped her map. Her heart leapt into her throat, pounding. Her hand closed around the can of pepper spray in her pocket.

A man stood in front of her. She hadn't heard him approach.

She should have taken Oreo. If only she'd taught him to stay quiet, but living alone, she'd encouraged his barking.

"Stay back," Anna commanded, but her voice came out as a squeak. "I'm armed."

The stranger smiled and lifted both of his arms, palms open. "I didn't mean to scare you." He wore proper hiking boots and had a blue rucksack strapped to his back.

Anna swallowed. "What do you want?"

10

"How long is the silent treatment going to last?" Chris asked, nibbling on an oatmeal bar. She stacked the remaining Tupperware containers on Anna's kitchen windowsill. At her feet, Oreo licked the crumbs off the kitchen floor, then sat and watched her chew, licking his lips.

Tom sat at the wooden table in the small dining room. The surface was cluttered with laptop parts and piles of tiny screws. Pressing his lips into a thin line, his tongue poking through every now and then, he tinkered with his computer.

"Can you fix it?" Chris asked.

Tom didn't reply. He'd ignored her all morning. With his brows furrowed, he removed another part from inside his laptop, studied the cables underneath and sighed. "If only I had the Internet."

He looked up and scowled upon noticing Chris' stare. He chewed on the inside of his cheek as if trying to convince himself to talk to her. Looking back at the laptop part he was holding in his hand, he flipped it over. "Is there a library nearby? Dad only taught me how to replace broken parts, not how to fix them."

Chris swallowed. He couldn't even look at her. When he

was younger, he'd always preferred her company over Lester's. Always stayed near her. Showered her with hugs and kisses. Now…

Chris forced herself to smile. "I doubt it's op—"

"You have your NHS badge." Tom pulled his mouth into a defiant pout. "Tell them you need books for work."

"I don't think I'll be going back to work."

Tom pressed his lips together but didn't reply. He placed the part gingerly onto the tablecloth, then reached for his screwdriver.

"Tom, please talk to me."

He sniffled and looked up. Bloodshot eyes met hers and her heart sank.

"I…" His voice cracked and he wiped his eyes with the back of his hand. "I don't understand how he's just…gone…"

"I know, sweetie. It's not your fault."

Tom scowled, eyes hardening. "You said that he wouldn't—"

Chris put down the oatmeal bar, rushed to his side and knelt in front of him, placing her hand on his thigh. He smelled of sweat. The way Lester had after a long day at work. "I'm sorry, Tom. I didn't know Dad would do this. I didn't know how sad he was and that's my fault. I didn't look after him."

Tom's bottom lip quivered. "Didn't he…didn't he love us enough?"

"Oh, sweetie, of course he did." She squeezed his thigh. "He loved us very much. Especially you. He was so proud of you. Sometimes…sometimes people just don't have the strength to hold on."

"You were with him. His blood is under your nails."

Chris balled her hand into a fist and closed her eyes. She'd scrubbed her nails, but the red remained stark against her pale fingers.

She'd lost an entire day. Left Tom's bedroom and walked into—

Hours she couldn't account for. Hours she must have spent staring at Lester's body.

She didn't remember...didn't remember if she'd passed out or just stood there.

But that didn't mean she'd hurt Lester. She would never—

The cat. Its popping eyes. The way her knife had slid into Mike's abdomen. The adrenaline surging through her body. The feeling of power coursing through her veins.

"Mum?"

Chris wiped her eyes. "I'm sorry. I loved your dad very much, and—"

"Sometimes you fought."

"Of course. All couples fight."

"You screamed at him for not helping around the house. For not doing enough."

"I know. I'm sorry." A lump grew in her throat and she swallowed. "I was frustrated—"

"He was ill."

Deflated, she bowed her head. "I'm sorry."

"What about me? Are you going to yell at me? Leave me behind? If I don't help enough?"

"Help with what?"

"I heard you talking to Anna last night."

Chris froze. Had he heard what she'd said about Lester? Her insides twisted, but Tom didn't seem to notice.

No. He wouldn't be talking to her if he knew.

Oreo had settled next to Tom's feet. Despite Tom's sulking, Oreo had taken an immediate liking to the boy. "You were talking about finding a farm, growing food, keeping animals." Tom absentmindedly patted the dog's head. "I don't know how to do any of that."

"You're thirteen, Tom. You don't *need* to know how to do any of that."

He didn't protest, didn't tell her that he was no longer a *boy* and almost fourteen now.

"I'm just…worried you'll…" His voice trailed off, his lower lip quivering.

"Oh, Tom." Chris gave his thigh another squeeze. "I'd never leave you behind."

His eyes softened, and she opened her arms in invitation, but he shook his head. A vast array of emotions flitted across his face. "How do you know Anna?"

Chris hesitated. Holding on to the table, she pulled herself to her feet and sat down on the chair opposite her son. At last, he was talking to her. "She's a friend. Why?"

"Do you trust her?"

Chris frowned. "Why do you ask?"

"You keep saying that desperate people are dangerous. What if we're in her way, somehow. This isn't a large flat." His brows knitted with worry. "What if her sister doesn't like us when she gets here?"

"Anna is a good person. She helped me the night…everything changed. She was the one who told me to stock up on supplies. She's the reason we have so much food and water. Besides, she left Oreo with us. She wouldn't trust us with her dog if she didn't like us, right?"

Tom clutched the screwdriver tightly, his knuckles white. "I don't get you. I've never heard of this Anna before and now—"

"Tom." Chris placed her hand on his arm, his muscles taut beneath her touch. The screwdriver shook in his hand. "You're getting yourself worked up over nothing."

"Why couldn't we go to James'?" His grimace hinted at a looming teenage tantrum. "You've known his parents for years."

"They live too far away."

Oreo pushed his nose against Tom's leg, then sat as if waiting for a treat. Tom broke off a small piece of Chris' half-eaten oatmeal bar and flicked it in the dog's direction. Oreo caught it in mid-air. "Good boy." He removed another screw from the laptop, then gathered them in a pile. "Can I come with you?"

"Where to?"

"You told Anna that you wanted to find more food."

"Oh."

"I'm hoping to find working electronics to salvage some of the parts." He grinned as if suddenly in his element. "Anything stored in a warehouse would have been turned off when everything went dark."

Chris frowned. This was not the first time he had mentioned they might find working electronic equipment. And the army had at least one functioning vehicle. "Go on?"

"Electronics that were switched on during the EMP are toast as well as anything connected to the grid." He imitated an exploding bomb with his hands. "Boom. Dead. But... anything that was turned off at the time might have survived. Even better if it didn't have batteries inside."

"But even if you found a working laptop. Even if...there's no Internet, and there's no way for you to charge the batteries. You may as well get used to pen and paper."

Tom grumbled. "Unless we find a generator."

"Those need fuel. Doesn't fuel go off eventually? Besides, even if it doesn't, we'd run out sooner rather than later."

"The one time somebody might actually be interested in my videos, and I can't even film or upload them."

"Anne Frank didn't have a computer either."

Tom stared at her and narrowed his eyes. "Haha. You're so funny."

"Look…I know you miss James, and perhaps once things have settled down—"

"Why not now? Anna is out there right now trying to find her sister. Why can't we do the same?"

Chris shrugged. "It's safe here. For now. I don't know how long the tinned goods across the country will last, but I don't think it'll even be a month. That's why I was thinking of the Poundland warehouse. If we can get some more food now, we can hide for longer. Either until they fix the electricity or until most people…" She cleared her throat. "Time is on our side. If we can hide and wait, we stand a chance."

"Won't everybody else just hide and wait as well?"

"Not if they don't have enough food and water at home."

Tom tilted his head and frowned. "Shouldn't we help others?"

"I don't think that'll be possible."

"But—"

"We have to take care of ourselves, Tom."

"You know James' dad owns a farm, don't you?"

Chris nodded. "Yes, but his dad lives half an hour away by car. The only reason those soldiers drove us here was because I work at the hospital. Besides, how do you know James is with his dad? He might be with his mum. And even if he is on the farm, don't his grandparents still live there? Does he have aunts and uncles? Cousins? How many people are potentially crammed into that house? What if they don't have space for us as well?"

"So…what's the plan?" Tom asked. "We just wait for people to die? Because to me it sounds like you want to swoop in right after they've died and take their stuff. You're scaring me."

"Tom?" She waited for him to look at her.

"Yes?"

"I'm trying to keep us safe. I'll have to make some tough

decisions in the coming weeks, and I need you to trust me, okay? Everything I do is to keep us safe."

He nodded.

"Now, if you really want to help me, let's take stock of what we have and then we need to plan a supply run."

CHRIS DIDN'T DOUBT for a second that dozens of soldiers were patrolling the shops in the town centre. Even if she managed to create a diversion and grab some supplies, she wouldn't be able to get away.

The Poundland warehouse, on the other hand, stood isolated on the edge of town. If the army had already emptied it, they probably wouldn't even bother guarding it.

With a bit of luck, they'd missed a crate or two filled with food among all the stationery and cleaning products.

Chris filled her first aid bag with cardboard. She eyed it, unconvinced. "Does this look as if I'm carrying important medical equipment?"

"Yes." Tom said, carrying the empty bucket from the bathroom to the balcony where it stood to collect rainwater. "I'm sorry, you can't use the loo until this has filled up again or you'll need to use bottled water to flush."

Chris rolled her eyes. "Thank you for the warning."

Ninety bottles of water stood along the walls of Anna's spare room. Enough drinking water for three months, especially if they continued to harvest and boil rainwater.

Food worried her a lot more. What they had wouldn't even last them four months. Not if Sarah joined them. And with Tom's appetite…

Anna had said that she'd hidden her food in little packages and not to worry about her, but Chris didn't trust anyone else with her sons' life and had searched the flat.

Anna hadn't been lying. She'd meticulously divided her supplies into neat packets which she'd stashed away in her wardrobe behind her clothes.

"Are you sure about going to Poundland, Mum?" Tom asked.

"I don't know…" Chris rubbed her face. "If we could hide for six months…"

"But what if we could hide for seven months…" Tom's voice trailed off as he stared at her.

"Exactly!"

"No. You don't understand what I'm saying. When will you be happy? You'll always want more. Eight months are better than seven and so on. It's dangerous out there. You said so yourself."

"It's now or never. If we don't go now, it'll be too late. Everything will be gone." She slapped her palm against the wall.

He took a step back. "Mum?"

"It'll be okay." She rubbed her burning hand. "Let's get ready."

Tom changed into black trousers and a white shirt, and Chris put on her scrubs.

"Good enough?" Tom asked, spinning once in front of her.

Pride filled her at the sight of her little baby looking all grown up. "Perfect." Chris smiled. "You were supposed to work as a porter at the hospital over the summer and decided to stay on and help because we're short-staffed."

"Won't they think I'm too young?"

"Act like you belong. Don't worry. They won't look too closely." Chris tied her hair back in a ponytail. "A soldier asked us to come to the warehouse. They said it was an emergency and to hurry." She shouldered the first aid bag. "We'll play it by ear."

Tom nodded, his cheeks flushed. His hair stuck to his sweaty forehead, and Chris patted his arm. "We'll be fine. Follow my lead."

She hung her lanyard with her NHS badge around her neck and adjusted her orange armband. There was nobody to be seen in the street when they left the block of flats.

"Where are the soldiers?" Tom whispered.

"Further up the road," Chris replied, pointing towards Sainsbury's. "They can't patrol *every* street. It wouldn't surprise me if they abandoned Harlow once they're done retrieving the food."

"I'm scared," he said so softly she almost couldn't make out the words.

"I know. Me too."

The walk took half an hour. It was warm despite the rain. Chris led them through the woods behind the hospital, bushes encroaching on the paths, and they had to step over thorny twigs to avoid tripping.

Emerging from the trees Chris stopped, looking up and down Fourth Avenue.

Without lorries thundering past, it was quiet, almost eerie. As if the world had suddenly ended, and they were left fighting to survive.

There was a smokehouse five minutes down the road that she'd often ordered ribs and wings from, and her stomach grumbled.

If they didn't find more food, hunger would be something she'd soon feel all the time.

"Let's go."

The industrial estate was quiet—birdsong and rain the only sound accompanying their footsteps.

Chris straightened her scrubs as they approached the warehouse. The metal gates stood open. Two young soldiers were leaning against it, smoking.

A tall, female soldier stepped forward. Chris' head barely reached the soldier's chest and she had to crane her neck to look into her eyes. "This is a restricted area."

"Bloody cheek to come here and beg for food," one of the soldiers muttered. Smoke streamed from his nostrils. "Join the queue like everybody else."

Chris' heart leapt into her throat. She bit back a curse. *This* was where they prepared the food crates for Harlow.

The warehouse had to be crawling with soldiers. But she couldn't give up now. Grabbing her badge, she shoved it in the female soldier's line of sight. "I was told that someone here is in need of assistance?"

The soldier groaned and waved for a colleague standing by one of the warehouse doors to come over. "Back to work," she barked at the two men still smoking.

A tall man shuffled over. He moved with a slight limp, one hand pressed against his lower back.

"Take the nurse inside. Find out who is injured and report back."

"Yes, ma'am." He turned to Chris and Tom. "Follow me."

Several buttons were missing on his uniform, and Chris could smell alcohol on his breath. He scratched his dark stubble, ambling into the warehouse. Chris frowned at the lack of discipline and wondered how long it would be before they abandoned their posts.

The air inside the warehouse was sticky and warm. A foul stench of rotting food clung to everything. Chris pulled the collar of her blouse over her mouth and nose.

Behind her, Tom retched.

"Breathe through your mouth," she hissed.

A group of soldiers stood in a corner, loading cardboard boxes with biscuits and tins of food. Chris had been right. This was no longer a warehouse. This was a distribution centre for the government.

And it was almost empty.

Chris swallowed, her gaze drifting over the dozens of empty shelves. "Just between you and me," she whispered to the limping soldier. "How many days before the food runs out?"

He snorted, then turned away from her. "Who here has called for a medic?"

Nobody replied.

Chris looked to Tom. She'd expected a few guards, not a warehouse full of soldiers. "Do you happen to remember the name of the injured man?" she asked, trying to buy herself some time.

Everyone was armed. She had to create a diversion somehow.

Tom shook his head. "I don't think they gave a name," he whispered, his eyes darting to the soldier's gun. "We should leave," he mouthed.

"No one?" the soldier yelled.

Chris flashed him her most cheerful smile and shrugged. "That's odd. Perhaps we misheard, and they meant for us to go somewhere else."

Tom darted forward and knocked his shoulder into one of the shelves, sending boxes flying. He took one and bolted.

"Stop him!" the soldier yelled, and everyone scrambled to their feet. Shouts filled the warehouse.

Tom raced off. Chris wanted to grab him and keep him safe, explain that it had all been a mistake, but he'd created the diversion she needed. She suddenly found herself alone and didn't know what to do.

After a moment's hesitation, she took action. She opened her bag, quickly discarded the cardboard and filled it with tins of spaghetti hoops—the nearest thing to hand.

That silly boy was risking his life. For them. For her.

Chris reached towards the shelf below. Soup—

Shots rang out. Somebody screamed.

Her heart leapt into her throat, and she fought down a surge of panic.

It wasn't Tom.

Her bag was bursting with heavy tins, but she forced it closed and darted back to the entrance. *Act like you belong. Don't hesitate.* She spotted the soldier with the limp and took a deep breath. "Excuse me?"

He jabbed his index finger in her direction. "You!" He ran a hand through his tousled hair. "You can't just—"

"I'm so sorry." She wrung her hands. "I didn't know he'd do that. Have you...have you caught him?"

"No."

She gritted her teeth to keep the expression on her face neutral. "I'll have to report this to the hospital, of course. We can't work with people like him. Would you like me to find out his address for you?"

The soldier nodded. "Please."

Dizziness overcame her as she spoke. "Everything is electronic nowadays, but as he's an intern he would have filled in a paper form. I'll check our archives and send you a report."

"Did you find the person who needed help?"

Chris shook her head. "Somebody must have thought it was funny to send a nurse on a fool's errand. Or we've come to the wrong place." She forced a laugh and patted her bag. "Right. I better bring this equipment back to the hospital."

"Do any of your machines still work?" the soldier asked, taking a step closer.

"No. What about yours?"

"A handful of vehicles. Mostly older ones. I don't know why. Perhaps something about where they'd been parked. Apart from that—" He shook his head. "Nothing."

"Thank you." Chris tried to look past him to see where Tom had run off to.

Another shot rang out.

The soldier laughed. "Oh, don't look so worried. He's the third one to try something like that this week. They'll get him."

Every fibre of her being wanted to break into a run and follow her son, but she forced herself to nod and smile. When he didn't say anything else, she walked away. Tears stung her eyes as she muttered prayers to herself.

Tom was fast. He was almost always reading these days, but football had kept him fit.

Once she was out of sight of the warehouse, Chris ran back to the flat. She tried not to slip in the puddles the rain had left behind, the strap of her heavy bag digging into her shoulder.

Were they chasing her?

She stopped and looked over her shoulder.

The road was empty.

She hurried the rest of the way back to the house. Once inside, she took the stairs two at a time and knocked, panting. "It's me." He had the keys. She wouldn't get inside without him.

Please be here. Please be here.

The door opened, and Tom's flushed face appeared. His expression was awash with relief the moment he saw her.

Chris hurried inside, dropped her bag and sank to her knees. Oreo licked her face, blissfully unaware of how close they'd come to losing everything.

Tom shut the door and exhaled.

Chris stroked Oreo's soft fur, the dog's warmth soothing her. Her arm throbbed where the bag had dug into her skin. "We can't ever do that again."

She'd almost lost Tom. She'd almost lost everything.

But she'd bought them another month.

11

Anna stood frozen in place, her heart hammering in her chest. The sound of her blood pumping in her ears was louder than the birds chirping in the surrounding trees, louder even than the crickets in the field.

It was all she could hear.

She pulled out her pepper spray and held it in front of her as if warding off vampires with a crucifix.

Without taking her eyes off the man in front of her, she scanned her environment. Horses grazed in the vast field beyond the road. A line of trees visible on the horizon.

She should have paid better attention to her surroundings, but the sight of the bodies had left her panicking.

Her grip on the pepper spray tightened, the blood draining from her hands. "Don't come any closer." Her voice came out raspy and small and she sounded more pleading than demanding. "What do you want?" Anna asked again. She pulled her shoulders back, lifting her chin to appear taller.

Less weak.

Less like prey.

The man smiled. He didn't move and kept his hands in the air where she could see them. "I'm not a threat."

He didn't appear to be carrying any weapons. "Where are you going?" he asked when she didn't reply.

Anna hesitated and bit her lip. "That's none of your business."

"It's best you avoid Braintree. The town is crawling with soldiers. One area attempted to defy martial law and stormed the streets."

Anna raised an eyebrow. "Why?"

"Beats me. They were gunned down without mercy. The soldiers hung the bodies from road signs all over town. Some form of morbid warning to the rest of us to stay inside."

Anna shuddered. "Surely, that's a…that can't…have they gone rogue?"

"Possibly." She met his warm, brown eyes and he nodded. "Avoid Braintree."

He appeared to be in his mid-forties with a trimmed beard that was streaked with grey. His weathered skin was tanned, and he wore his brown hair in a messy bun.

A wave of nausea washed over Anna at his words. It hadn't even been two weeks and already—

"I'm on my way to Colchester." Anna didn't lower the pepper spray, her eyes never leaving the stranger.

"I can be your guide if you'd like. I know my way around this area."

Her chest tightened. How could she say no without offending him? What if he insisted on following her? "Why?"

"I live here."

"I'd assumed as much, but why would you want to be my guide, and what makes you think that I would willingly follow a stranger?"

"I'm Bob. Nice to meet you." He laughed and a mischievous twinkle appeared in his eyes. "There you go. I'm no longer a stranger."

Anna scowled. "I don't think that's a very funny joke, Bob."

He shrugged. "My wife says that a lot."

"Look, if I stay on the A120—"

"You don't want to stay on the A120. There's a roadblock just before the Braintree exit." He tucked a strand of brown hair behind his ear. "I can guide you through these fields until you can safely get back onto the road. What do you have to lose?"

A whole lot. But her heartbeat was slowly returning to normal and she lowered her pepper spray. "I don't know, Bob. What *do* I have to lose? It's not even been two weeks and soldiers in Braintree are stringing citizens from road signs. I fully expect to find some people have bypassed the food supply scheme entirely and gone straight to cannibalism."

He snorted. "You read a lot of fiction, don't you?"

Anna blushed and shrugged. "I mean…"

"I get it. You need to be careful. But not everyone you come across can possibly be a villain, right?" He brushed some dried grass from his trouser legs. "No cannibalism here. I promise. I like to keep fit and walk twenty miles a day. I'm out here a lot, and I know the fields like the back of my hand. Keeps me on my toes, keeps me healthy and keeps me fed." He opened his bag and tilted it so she could see its contents. "I lay traps to catch rabbits. My wife cooks them over an open fire in our garden."

"How do you know how to do that?" Anna asked, staring at the dead rabbit in Bob's bag. She shuddered.

"My grandfather used to hunt. He taught me."

"What are you and your wife going to do?"

"We'll grow food and hunt. Apart from that, we'll keep fit and wait. If Braintree is any indication most people will be dead within the first six months."

"You reckon?"

"I'm still hoping the government can fix the national grid, but it's been over a week. They'll kill each other over basic supplies before starving. Disease will mop up the rest."

"And then?"

Bob pointed east. "How about we walk while we talk? I don't like staying in the same place for long. You never know." He set out without checking to see if she was following him.

She frowned, spotting the big knife tucked into his belt.

Anna scratched her head. She could run away now that he wasn't looking, but if he really wanted to hurt her, she wouldn't get far anyway. Her feet screamed in agony—her knee nothing but a painful knot.

Bob's calves on the other hand, were almost the circumference of her thighs.

He'd catch her in no time.

She decided she might as well follow the man and quickened her steps to catch up with him. He was muttering to himself. His voice sounded oddly calming.

"...gather other people together. Build something."

"You don't think the government will restore the power? Maintain the peace?"

"Not if they insist on hanging people to make a point." He chuckled dryly. "No. They'll run out of food before they'll restore power. They'll lose control before the end of July."

"Hmm." Anna had to struggle to keep up with his pace.

Bob didn't seem to notice as he continued talking. "I think small settlements will form. Neighbours who help each other out. Perhaps they'll manage to restore small pockets of electricity powered by the sun or the wind. And in a few years, ten to fifteen perhaps, smaller settlements will come together and form a village. And so on…" His voice trailed off as he stepped over the thick trunk of a fallen tree. He turned, offering Anna his hand.

She took it and climbed over the trunk. "What about the Queen?"

Bob snorted. He stopped and rubbed his forehead as if contemplating her question. "The family might survive. They have big enough estates to hide from the public and probably a bunker full of supplies or something. But I doubt they can come back and...what...claim we're still their subjects?" He puffed out his chest and his voice shifted. "It's been eighty-four years, and I just wanted to let you know I'm Prince George, and this is my country." His Essex accent had disappeared entirely, but he still sounded nothing like the Royal Family.

Anna grinned. "I'm Anna. Thank you for helping me."

He shook her hand. "Not everyone is a reprobate, right? There must be decent people out there. People like you."

Anna winced. Was she a decent person? She'd stolen from a supermarket mere hours after the power had gone out. Taken everything she'd needed without thinking of anyone else.

She didn't consider that *decent.*

You've helped Chris, a voice in her head piped up as if trying to make her feel better but the guilt still lingered.

And when her neighbour had been shot, she'd immediately raided his flat.

But you shared the food and water you found.

"I'm not sure I'd consider myself a *decent* person."

"I'd argue that the rules have changed," Bob said. "We need to survive. And what we have to do in order to survive has changed since the EMP."

"Do you know what happened?"

"My wife thinks it was a CME."

"A C—what?"

"CME. Coronal Mass Ejection. We'd had a period of unusually strong solar activities during the days before the EMP, and even a few solar flares.

"What's the difference between a solar flare and a coronary—a CME?"

He chuckled. "Coronal Mass Ejection. It's basically a shock wave travelling towards the Earth. I don't really know how it works, but my wife insists that that's what it was. It's her hobby. Stargazing."

"The sun's turned on us?" Anna snorted. "No war? No invasion? No enemies trying to take over our country?"

"Not according to my wife, but how would we know? Perhaps they're in London, but I doubt it. I don't think the army would bother with *Braintree* if we were under attack."

"Fair point. They'd definitely not bother with Harlow."

They arrived at the edge of the field, and Bob led them along a narrow pathway trailing through the thicket. He pushed a thorny branch aside, waiting for Anna to pass. He smelled of soap and fresh sweat. She darted past him and mumbled a thank you.

He walked behind her now, and an image of him sticking his knife into her back invaded her mind. But she reminded herself once again that he would have hurt her already if he'd wanted to.

"There's the A120," Bob said, pointing at the road visible in the distance. "Stick to the left side of the field until you can't see the town anymore. The dual carriageway will lead you to Colchester. It'll be crawling with soldiers just like Braintree, so be careful." He smiled. "I hope you'll find whatever it is you're looking for."

Anna nodded. "Thank you, Bob."

"And if you ever need a place to stay, I walk around these fields at least once a day. Who knows…perhaps I'll even make a start on one of those settlements?"

She smiled and waved.

"Anna?"

"Yes?"

"You said you don't think you're a decent person. Do you think it's possible to spot evil?"

"What do you mean?"

"I could have been a cannibal. I could have kidnapped you. Hurt you. Or you could have hurt me. I don't know what you carry in that bag of yours, and I let you walk behind me. I don't think women are harmless, but I also doubt all men you'll meet will be good people. So…how do you spot evil? How do you identify the ones who will hurt you?"

"I don't know," Anna said. "I can tell you why I don't think I'm a decent person. It was almost midnight when my TV screen went black. Several cars had broken down in the middle of the road. I checked my own car, then, without hesitating, I rushed to the nearest Tesco and took home food and water for three months. With the tills not working, there was no way for me to pay. That's called looting."

"Some might say that's called being smart."

"Where do you draw the line?"

Bob shrugged. "Hurting others without just cause. If I invite people into my home…how will I know that they won't take everything they need and leave me for dead?"

"Invite people you already know?"

"Everyone I know lives miles away."

"Sounds like you should have talked to your neighbours more." Anna laughed and turned to walk away. A small part of her was still worried he'd follow and hurt her, but she didn't want to look over her shoulder and make him think she didn't trust him.

She quickened her pace and made her way towards the road.

HER SISTER'S house was located on the outskirts of Colchester. The area appeared abandoned. Several houses had burnt down, leaving nothing but blackened, jagged remains of walls.

Black smoke rose above the town centre.

Sarah's house was still standing, but the windows at the front had shattered. The curtains were drawn.

Her sister's Renault was parked in the driveway. A crack ran down the middle of the windscreen.

Anna knocked.

No response.

She retrieved the key from underneath the flowerpot next to the front door and unlocked the side gate to let herself into the garden. The spare key to the house was taped to the bottom of a wooden birdhouse next to the patio.

Anna let herself in.

A musty odour lingered in the air. Dust tickled Anna's nose and she sneezed.

The smell reminded her of coming home after a holiday. After the house had been unoccupied for days.

Her stomach sank.

"Sarah?"

She found a note on the kitchen table.

Anna! I've gone to Harlow and I'll wait for you in your flat. If for any reason your flat isn't safe, meet me at sunrise where Mum used to take us every Sunday morning.

Anna smiled. Pet's Corner. The local petting zoo. Her sister was clever.

She tested the tap just in case things were different out here. Brown sludge dripped thickly into the sink.

Anna sat down and took off her shoes, inspecting her blisters. She found plasters and disinfectant wipes and cleaned them up.

Her feet were howling at the prospect of having to walk another forty miles.

She felt exhausted and decided to get a good night's sleep before making her way back.

Hopefully, Sarah would be waiting for her.

Hopefully, they'd all be safe and together again soon.

12

CHRIS WOKE WITH A START. THE MOON WAS VISIBLE THROUGH the blinds, hanging low and bright over the local park like a thick silver plate.

She sat up and peered out the window, rubbing the sleep from her eyes. A grey, horizontal streak over the horizon announced the sunrise.

Something had woken her up. An unfamiliar noise.

Tom snored softly next to her, his tousled hair curling at the neck.

There. Again.

The door to the spare room stood open a crack.

"Oreo?"

A growl was the only response. It turned into a low rumble, then a bark.

Somebody was walking up the stairs. A stranger.

Chris shook Tom's shoulders and pressed her index finger to her lips. "Shhh! Wake up. There's someone in the building."

"What?" Tom mumbled, then yawned.

Chris grabbed her pepper spray from the bedside table,

tilted her head and listened. The pitter-patter of dog feet on the wooden floor was followed by another bark.

"Are you sure it's not just a neighbour?" Tom asked, sitting up.

Chris fumbled for a candle, lit it and shuffled into the hallway, gripping her pepper spray. The candlelight reflected in Oreo's eyes. They glowed red in the dark.

"What is it, boy?" Chris whispered. She bent down to stroke him when someone knocked on the door. Oreo pulled up his lips, revealing his sharp teeth and snarled.

The handle turned. Rattled.

Tom shuffled into the hallway, a blanket wrapped around his shoulders. "What the—"

The door burst open.

Bright light filled the hallway, and Chris squeezed her eyes shut. A torch? Her heart pounded. Wincing, she opened one eye.

Oreo darted forward in a mock attack, his barking high-pitched.

Blinking rapidly, her vision adjusted. A soldier stood in the door, both his assault rifle and his torch pointed straight at them.

"Both of you where I can see you," the man ordered. "Is there anybody else in the flat?"

Chris shook her head.

"What about the woman who lives here? Mid-thirties. Tall with dark blonde hair. Large nose."

"Anna?"

"I don't know her name. Is she here?"

"No," Chris whispered.

The soldier lowered his torch. "Stay right where you are." He walked down the hallway, shining his torch into every room.

Oreo cowered as the soldier walked past, his barking

incessant. The soldier gestured towards Oreo with the barrel of his rifle. "Make the dog shut up. Now."

Tom led Oreo into Anna's bedroom and closed the door. "I can't stop him barking, but he won't hurt you. Please don't shoot him."

The soldier glowered at Tom, then pointed to the living room. "Sit in there. Keep your hands where I can see them."

Chris tried to slide the pepper spray back into her trouser pocket, but the soldier took a step towards her and pointed the torch straight at her torso. "What are you hiding?"

"Nothing."

"Drop it."

She considered emptying the pepper spray into his face. If she dropped her candle, it might distract him long enough for her to get his eyes, but his assault rifle was aimed at her son.

If he accidentally fired it…

With no choice, Chris dropped the can. It fell onto the wooden floor with a loud thud. She peered past the soldier, looking for his backup. Was he alone?

"Sit," the soldier barked, and she flinched.

They shuffled into the living room. Chris sank down into the sofa cushions next to Tom and took his trembling hand. "It'll be okay," she whispered, placing the candle on the coffee table.

Oreo's barks were muffled and sporadic. *He's more likely to bark and hide than bite.* Anna had been right. He hadn't attacked, instead he'd cowered. He must have smelled their fear. So much for the dog helping guard the flat.

"Light the other candles," the soldier said to Tom.

Tom obeyed, his hand shaking as he lit the candles on the coffee table with a match. Once the flames stopped flickering, the soldier placed his torch on the floor. Tom blew out the match and Chris watched the black smoke curl in the candlelight.

She was trained for this.

She'd handled aggressive patients.

She could handle a single soldier.

"What do you want from us?" she asked. "We haven't done anything wrong." Had somebody tracked Tom from the Poundland warehouse? Her heart was racing. Would they arrest him?

"The woman who lives here…Anna. Did she leave to find her sister?"

Chris exhaled. He wasn't here for her son. "How do you know about Anna's sister?" A flicker of hope was ignited in her belly and for a moment Chris thought that perhaps he was a family friend. Somebody who cared for Anna. Somebody who wouldn't be a danger after all.

"She told me," the soldier said. "She also told me that the army wouldn't manage to keep the peace, and that there wasn't enough food for everyone. And she was right. London has descended into chaos. The Prime Minister has fled to York." He rubbed his face, and Chris' hopes were shattered.

He had the face of a desperate man.

"How long have you known Anna?" Chris asked, trying to buy time. He couldn't hurt them if he was busy talking. Her gaze darted across the room and settled on the lamp by the television. Its base would be heavy enough to knock him out. If she could grab it and strike—

His finger was on the trigger.

The barrel of his rifle aimed at Tom's head.

"I don't know her," he said with a shrug. "She asked if I could get a message to Colchester when I was on patrol the other day. That was the extent of our relationship." His eyes drifted over her and Tom, cold and hard.

Chris swallowed, her mouth had gone dry and her tongue felt sticky. "Why are you here?"

"The morning after the grid went down our squad was

drafted in to help distribute supplies. I left my frightened wife and son at home so I could do my job." A small smile tugged at the corners of his mouth. "He's two months old today. My superiors promised to look after my family, but after what Anna said, I abandoned my post to check on them. I walked for days. By the time I made it home, my wife was so stressed, she couldn't breastfeed, and they didn't have any formula left. My son...he was starving...feverish."

Chris frowned, mimicking his expression. Sometimes mirroring emotions did the trick and established empathy. She gestured for him to go on.

Tears glistened in his eyes, but his features hardened. "I asked my superiors to let my wife and son see a doctor. They refused. I asked for formula. They said they'd run out. It's not even been two weeks and they've *already* run out. Our warehouses are empty." He fell silent, wiping his brow with the back of his hand.

"I'm sorry," Chris whispered. *Every man for himself,* Mike had said. "Did you find any formula?"

"They told me that my wife had failed to sign up to the food supply scheme." The soldier scoffed, the barrel of his weapon dropping slightly. "She was too exhausted to queue, and our neighbours wouldn't help her."

"That's awful," Chris said. She squeezed Tom's hand, felt the rapid pulse in his wrist. "What's your name?" she asked the soldier, thinking of her training. Build an emotional connection. Establish trust and empathy. She needed him to see her and Tom as equals. Human beings worthy of survival. Just like him.

He'd be far less likely to hurt them if he—

But the soldier shook his head. Almost violently. "You don't need to know my name." His voice was hard, uncaring.

She still didn't know why he was here.

Did he think Anna had formula? Did he think she was a doctor?

"My name is Chris," she said softly. "And this is my son, Tom." She was desperate for him to understand that they too were suffering. Needed food. Wanted to survive.

Deserved to survive.

The soldier didn't acknowledge her and continued speaking as though she hadn't said a word. "A man down the road took pity on us and gave us a box of formula, said he had enough for a few months. He told me his brother had fled London and that they were planning on moving further north." He frowned, narrowing his eyes. "A few nights ago, I sat with my wife and remembered Anna's words."

"Anna's words?"

"She asked me if I was looking after my own family. If I was prepared for the coming famine. I laughed at her." He paused and took a deep breath. "She claimed that the army was just there to keep the public from storming the supermarkets and warehouses and that the food was being stockpiled for the rich and powerful." He scratched his nose and sniffled. "She was right."

"Sounds like something that Anna would say."

"She talked like someone who was prepared, you know? Like someone who would have a flat full of food." His eyes narrowed, and the grip on his rifle tightened.

The candles flickered as he stood.

"Show me the kitchen," he said to Chris. "You"—he pointed his chin at Tom—"don't move!"

It was a warm and humid night. Sweat had gathered below her hairline, trickling down her neck. The stench of fear filled the room. Chris rubbed her forehead and thought of ways to save them. Save their food.

He was definitely alone. He'd even admitted to abandoning his post. That made him a deserter.

If both she and Tom attacked at the same time, they might be able to overpower him, but would Tom help her kill him?

Would he—

He has to.

This was no world for children, and the sooner he learned how to kill, the sooner he'd learn to always do what was necessary.

He had to grow up.

But at least one of them would be dead if the soldier moved first. If he shot his gun. Chris wasn't prepared to risk Tom's life.

She shuffled into the kitchen.

Even if she managed to kill him—what would they do with his body? Anna had said that two flats in the block were empty, but the smell—

"Move!" The cold metal of his rifle dug into her back. "Looks like I wasn't wrong." Chris heard the grin in his voice. "This is enough food to last us months."

Chris turned, lifting her chin defiantly. "These are our supplies. My family has the right to survive. That's my son in the other room. He's only thirteen. He deserves to live."

The soldier shrugged. "I joined the army to protect people, but I can't save everyone. I'm sorry, but I can't. And since I'm the one with the gun…"

Anger bubbled in her stomach. He was the second man in a short period of time who believed himself to be the new sheriff in town simply because he was armed. Mike had been the first, and she'd killed him.

She wouldn't let this soldier take their food. "Doesn't it bother you? That you're no longer protecting people?"

"I was naïve. I thought the government would fix this mess. I didn't realise how low our stocks were. How quickly warehouses and supermarkets would empty. There are over fifty million people in England. We can't feed them all.

They'll starve. It's inevitable. It's every man for himself now."

"Please let us keep at least some of it. Perhaps we can share?" She spoke slowly to hide the terror choking her.

He didn't reply, but his left eye twitched.

"Take half? If you take half, both our families stand a chance." She took a deep breath, gathering all her courage. "If you don't agree to that, my son will run." She spoke loudly so Tom would hear. "He'll make a run for it, and he will be screaming for help out there. He'll come back with your mates, and they won't be kind to you."

He narrowed his eyes.

"You've abandoned your post. You're a deserter. And you're trying to harm civilians. I know you believe it won't be long before we'll shoot each other in the streets over scraps, but at least for now, they won't tolerate what you're doing."

"If he runs, I'll shoot you."

Chris squared her jaw. "Even so, my son will be safe."

"I'll tell them you were hoarding supplies and that—"

"It's not illegal to have food at home. We didn't sign up to the food supply scheme. My son will be safe, but you won't be able to go back to your wife and son. They won't let you." She bit her lip. "I'm offering you half."

His features remained motionless as he stared at her.

Calculations were going through her mind at a rapid pace. Even if he only took half, they'd be in trouble. Especially if Anna came back with her sister. The food wouldn't last for more than two months.

But they'd be safe. For now.

"When is Anna coming back?" the soldier asked. "I liked her. She helped me."

"Soon, hopefully. That is her dog you can hear barking."

"Mum?" Tom's voice shook.

The soldier's head snapped up, looking towards the hallway. He took a step back so he could see both the hallway and Chris. His finger found the trigger. "Stay where you are, kid. If I hear you move, I'll shoot your mum."

"Half," Chris repeated.

He grimaced. "Fine. I'll leave you half. For Anna. There's a bag by the door. Fill it. Some of everything."

Chris slowly walked down the hallway. Her stomach knotted with fear. She'd failed to keep Tom safe. Had failed to guard the flat. She'd fallen asleep instead of keeping watch. Had missed Oreo's barking.

She grabbed his bag and set it down on the kitchen counter. Rummaging through the jars of rice and cereal, she poured half of everything into freezer bags.

And now this man knew how much food they had.

And if he changed his mind, he'd be back for the rest—perhaps with friends.

Her stomach sank at the thought.

This flat was no longer safe.

When he finally left, she closed what was left of the front door and sank to the floor, her back to it. Her shoulders shook as sobs wracked her body.

"Mum?" Tom rushed over and wrapped his arms around her. She buried her face in his neck and let the tears flow freely. Oreo whined, approaching with his head hanging low, the whites of his eyes showing.

Tom patted his head soothingly. "Mum? What do we do now?"

"We continue. We survive. There's still all that food in Anna's wardrobe."

"But what if he comes back?"

Chris hesitated and closed her eyes. Then a whisper: "I don't think he will."

Had she done the right thing?

She brushed a strand of hair from Tom's face and smiled. "We'll be fine."

"How do you know he won't come back?"

"Because…" She stood with her son's help and walked back into the kitchen to put the empty jars at the back of the cupboard. "Because I've crumbled rat poison into his cereal."

Chris lay on the bed with her eyes closed, a sheet draped loosely over her lower body. Outside, the birds were chirping away.

A strong breeze had brought with it some cooler weather, and the blinds were clattering against the window frame.

She hadn't slept since the soldier had left. Tom had offered to stay up and take a watch to guard the flat, but Chris had refused.

Tom was now sitting in the armchair near the window reading his programming book. The only noise in the flat was the occasional rustle whenever he turned the page.

Oreo lay at his feet.

A shot rang out in the distance. The third she'd heard that morning.

Twelve days since the world had gone dark and already the end was beginning.

"Tom?"

He didn't reply, didn't even look up.

"Are you okay?" She didn't know what else to say. It didn't matter whether she'd done the right thing. Her son thought she was a monster.

Death had invaded their lives, lurking around every corner.

She didn't even know the soldier's name.

Ingesting rat poison was a horrific way to die. Horrible

stomach cramps would be the first indication that something was wrong. He'd bleed to death, never knowing why. Along with his family if he'd taken the food back to them. *Serves him right.*

"We don't have enough food." Chris flinched at the venom lacing Tom's voice. His tone was defiant, but she could hear tears through his anger.

"We still have Anna's—"

"She's bringing back her sister. There'll be four of us, mum."

"I'm painfully aware of that, but he had a gun, and I couldn't stop him."

Tom huffed and buried his nose back in his book.

Oreo got to his feet and wagged his tail. He whined, pushing his nose against Tom's hand. With his ears pricked and his mouth open, he looked as if he was smiling. As if he was trying to tell them something.

Chris froze and listened.

Somebody was in the stairwell.

Jumping to her feet, she grabbed the carving knife resting on the bedside table. She'd sharpened it after the soldier had left.

"Wait here." She dashed into the hallway.

They'd pushed a chest of drawers in front of the broken door. They had to push and pull it every time Oreo needed to be let out and it had scratched the wooden floor.

Oreo followed behind her, his feet pattering across the floor. He spun around and barked once, tail wagging. It sounded friendly.

Was it Anna?

A knock.

Chris held her breath.

Another knock.

Tom appeared in the doorway to the spare room. "Is it Anna?"

"Shhh."

A shuffle followed by a muffled voice. "Hello? Anna? Are you there?"

Chris' stomach dropped. It had to be Sarah. Anna's sister. Chris held her index finger up to her lips. "Let me think," she mouthed.

"Mum?"

"We don't have enough food."

He scowled. "It's Anna's sister."

Another knock. "Hello? I can hear you whispering. Who are you? Where is Anna? Why are you in her flat?"

Chris pressed her knuckles into her eyes. If it were just herself and Tom, she could stretch the food. Make it last.

They could hide.

Wait it out.

Would Sarah believe her if she told her that Anna had left and wouldn't be back? Would she give up and walk away? Or would she wait?

Once Anna came back, she'd find Sarah outside her flat, and her sister would tell her that Chris hadn't let her in.

The soldiers might help them, and they were armed.

A horrible thought came to her, and she barely dared consider it. It loomed at the edges of her mind, still and terrifying. Chris closed her eyes and contemplated it.

The thought took shape and her throat grew dry with apprehension.

She'd killed people in self-defence.

This time it wouldn't be.

Then again…wasn't it to protect her son?

Once Anna came back, she'd tell her that her sister had never shown up. She'd make her a cold coffee and comfort her.

"Mum?"

Anna would never know.

Chris lifted her head to find her son's eyes filled with concern.

Fists pounded on the door. "Hello? Please tell me if my sister is okay?"

Chris took a deep breath and pushed the chest of drawers out of the way.

She could do this.

She was strong enough to survive.

13

Anna wasn't sure if it had been ten or eleven days since the EMP. She'd tried to mark each day in her notebook but had forgotten to do so at least once, possibly twice. Not even two weeks later, and she'd already lost the last bit of normality.

She'd slept for more than twelve hours, and upon waking had discovered it was already late afternoon. Her sister's sheets smelled of her and despite missing Oreo, the scent had been comforting.

She was desperate for a hot bath to soak her aching knee.

Opening her sister's wardrobe, she found a dry shirt and a pair of socks before putting on her rain jacket.

She opened her notebook.

Sarah! I was here but you'd already left. I'll meet you back in Harlow.

Tearing the page from her notebook, she placed it on the kitchen table, weighing it down with what used to be Sarah's fruit bowl. It was empty save for a few fruit flies walking along the rim as if waiting for a top-up.

She locked the door and taped the key to the birdhouse before locking the gate. The air was thick with the stench of smoke. She coughed, covering her mouth and nose with a scarf. The dense smoke was black, covering her skin in soot.

Forty miles lay ahead of her.

Her right knee had grown to twice the size of her left one, throbbing painfully. She'd hoped a good night's sleep would fix it. *So much for that.*

The humidity wasn't helping.

Anna thought of Bob and how he'd kept fit by walking twenty miles every day.

Well, it was too late for that now.

This time, Anna walked through the night and didn't stop to rest. It had to be more comfortable than trying to sleep on a bench in damp clothes.

She took one step after another. Then another. And another.

The thought of seeing Sarah again kept her on her feet.

If only she'd waited a little longer in her flat before embarking on this journey, but she hadn't been able to shake the image of Sarah bleeding out somewhere.

Waiting for Anna to come to her rescue.

Just like she always had.

After their mum had died, Sarah had been confronted with their father's true nature. Anna had offered Sarah her spare room to get away from their father but buried in grief, Sarah had refused, unable to let go of the house she'd grown up in.

The house their mum had died in.

Suddenly, she'd borne the brunt of their father's narcissism.

As her world collapsed, Sarah had lashed out. Had destroyed every friendship she'd ever had, and along the way, every relationship Anna had ever had as well.

She'd stumbled from one party to the next, too drunk to remember most nights, and it had been Anna who had to pick her up every time she'd been too intoxicated to call a cab and who had to hold her hair back when she used to throw up after.

David, Anna's first long-term partner, had been a lovely guy, but after two years he refused to put up with both Sarah's antics and Anna's refusal to give up on her sister, ruining any future Anna might have had with him.

It took Sarah years to finally grow up. Anna had met Dan not long after, and Sarah promised to behave.

Apprehensive, yet hopeful, Anna had told her, "You're more important than any relationship could ever be."

Anna had never found out what triggered the change in her sister, but Sarah had climbed the career ladder and finally bought herself a house, and Anna had moved in with Dan.

"Isn't it time for you to find your own boyfriend?" Anna had jokingly asked the day after Sarah signed the mortgage agreement.

"I don't want to meet someone only to find out he's like Dad," Sarah had replied.

"They're not all like Dad, you know."

"I loved him. I loved him so much and he just—"

"What about women?" Anna had asked.

"I'm not attracted to women."

Raising her glass, Anna had chuckled. "Here's to being single forever."

"To being single forever."

After everything they'd been through together, after taking Sarah to the hospital to have her stomach pumped, after picking her up from the police station, Anna would never forgive herself if her sister was lying dead in a ditch somewhere.

It was late morning by the time she returned to Harlow. She'd kept to the main roads, hidden by darkness. She'd walked for almost fifteen hours if not longer. Her knee and hip were two distinct knots of pain by the time she crossed the river near the train station.

Fifth Avenue appeared abandoned.

Relief washed over her as she approached her block of flats. She stopped and hid behind an abandoned car, peering up the street, inhaling deeply. The smell of smoke was faint, unlike in Colchester.

The soldiers had moved further up towards Sainsbury's. They'd set up another roadblock. No one was coming in or getting out of the town centre that way.

Gritting her teeth against the pain in her knee, Anna ran the last few feet. Sweat was pouring off her, but she didn't stop. She knew what the soldiers were capable of doing—she'd seen it happen first-hand.

Entering her building, she stopped near the door of the ground floor flat and listened.

Silence.

She raised her hand to knock and lowered it again.

Had her neighbours with the toddler left?

She knew the other flats were empty. The bald man from the second floor—Anna shook her head and closed her eyes.

The gunshot still echoed in her ears. The dark spot on the tarmac flashed before her eyes. Anna wiped her face with her shirt. Sweat stained the fabric a dirty yellow.

Perhaps she could ask Chris and Tom to move into one of the other flats? Together, they could defend the building.

She rushed up the stairs as quickly as she could with her throbbing knee. She heard Oreo whine the moment she reached the top floor and grinned. "Have you been a good boy?" she asked through the door. She heard him spinning around with excitement in response.

That's when she noticed the door was splintered around the lock. It looked like somebody had kicked it open. She tried her key, but it wouldn't turn.

Anna knocked. "Hello? Chris? It's me."

She pressed her ear against the damaged door. Oreo's whining grew louder. Had something happened to Chris and Tom? Had they left?

No. The door wouldn't be locked or barricaded from the inside. "Hello? Chris?"

She swallowed the sour taste filling her mouth. Why wasn't Chris letting her in? She pulled on the door handle, rattling it. She shouldn't have trusted a stranger. How stupid of her.

Anna pounded on the door.

Oreo was inside.

Her food and medicine. Her clothes! "Chris? Tom?"

She heard shuffling behind the door. Whispering was followed by a groan as something heavy was shifted and dragged across the floor.

Then finally, the door opened a crack and Chris pulled her inside. "You're back."

"What has happened to the door?" Anna asked, bending down to scratch behind Oreo's ears. "Were you attacked? Did someone break in?"

She looked over Chris' shoulder. Tom stood in the doorway to the spare room, his eyes hollow and haunted, his face pale.

"We're okay," Chris said.

Anna's chest of drawers stood next to the front door. Judging by the scratches in the wooden floor it had been moved more than once. "What's—"

"We were robbed."

"Robbed?" Anna bent down and massaged her knee. Oreo helpfully licked the sweat off her calves. She looked down the hallway. Where was her sister? Had Sarah not made it?

"That soldier you told us about. The one who shot your neighbour. He broke in and took half of our supplies."

Anna gasped. John. She remembered his face only too well. The way his eyes had narrowed before he'd lifted his gun and killed her downstairs neighbour. "He took half?"

"He was going to take everything, but he remembered you and said he owed you. And…I may have threatened him a tiny bit."

"He owed me?"

Chris wrinkled her nose and pointed at the bathroom door. "You look dreadful. You should get washed and changed. There's fresh water in there." Chris pulled a clean shirt from the washing basket near Anna's bedroom door and threw it to her. "No offence but—"

"I stink. I know. Is Sarah not here?"

"No. Didn't you find her? Wasn't she in Colchester?"

Tom grunted and disappeared into the living room.

Anna frowned, then turned her attention back to Chris. "No. She'd left by the time I got to Colchester. There was a note. She said she'd wait here."

Anna's thighs trembled from exhaustion as she entered the bathroom. Her knee throbbed. She took off her trousers and inspected her leg. It was blotchy and her skin itched from the dirt. She used baby wipes and fresh water to clean herself. It wasn't as good as a hot shower, but by the time she put on new clothes, she felt more like herself again.

Robbed. Half their supplies gone. And *where* was Sarah?

It didn't make sense that she wasn't here.

She put on deodorant and sniffed herself before giving herself a quick once-over in the mirror.

Chris waited on the sofa in the living room. Tom sat by the radiator. Oreo had settled with his head on Tom's lap.

"You weren't hurt?" Anna asked.

"No."

"Tell me what happened?"

"He burst through the door two nights ago. Alone. He had

an assault rifle and forced us to sit on the sofa. You were right about Oreo. The poor thing cowered in your room. The soldier said that after you'd warned him, he abandoned his post and went home to his wife and baby."

"He has a baby?"

Chris nodded. "His wife had run out of formula by the time he came home, and the baby was sick."

"Are you worried he'll come back for more? Is that why you barricaded the front door?"

Chris fell silent. Tom stopped scratching Oreo's ear and her dog whined. The boy stared off into space, his mind obviously elsewhere. His eyes were bloodshot.

"What's wrong?" Anna asked him.

"He's just tired," Chris said. "He hasn't slept since the break-in."

Tom scowled.

"Why don't you go and have a lie-down?"

He grunted in reply and shuffled out of the room. Moments later, a door slammed.

Anna flinched.

Silence filled the room. Chris chewed on her lip. "I doubt that soldier will be back," she whispered. "I crumbled rat poison into his cereal. I just…I didn't know what else to do."

Anna swallowed. "Wow."

"He threatened us with a gun. Just like you said, I was worried he'd change his mind and come back for the rest." She scratched her head. "I couldn't risk it."

Anna didn't reply.

Chris laughed nervously. "Let's not talk about this anymore. It's done. How about you? It looked like you were limping. Were you hurt?"

"It's just my knee," Anna said. "I can't believe Sarah hasn't made it." She slumped down on the sofa. Oreo jumped up and settled against her legs. Her gaze darted around the room. Nothing had been moved. Everything looked just like it had when she left.

Apart from the front door.

"So many days wasted. And now we've lost half our food." Anna rubbed her face. Tom's reaction worried her. He'd been through a lot, but why was he so sullen?

Silence filled the room, and Chris wouldn't meet her eyes. The tension was palpable.

Something was wrong.

Sarah had promised she'd wait for her here.

Things weren't adding up, and she didn't really know Chris. The woman with the bitter lines around her mouth. The woman who'd told her husband that she wished he'd just end it all. The woman who didn't hesitate to poison a stranger.

Anna shivered.

What was she going to do now?

14

CHRIS HAD OFFERED TO SLEEP AND KEEP WATCH BY THE FRONT door. She'd pumped up an air mattress, settling by the chest of drawers.

Anna had tossed and turned for a while, her worries keeping her awake, but exhaustion had won, and she'd slept for almost twenty-four hours. When she woke up, she found Oreo at her feet, curled up in a ball.

If for any reason your flat isn't safe, meet me at sunrise where Mum used to take us every Sunday morning.

Anna peeked through the blinds. It was gone midday. Why sunrise? What was wrong with sunset? She'd have to stay awake to get to Pet's Corner early enough.

Sarah had said she'd make her way to Anna's flat, but she wasn't here. Either her sister had decided that the flat wasn't safe, or she'd been hurt—or worse.

If her sister had decided the flat wasn't safe, had Sarah knocked?

Had she met Chris?

But why wouldn't Chris have let her in?

Anna stretched, massaging her knee. Oreo yawned. "I

wish you could speak." She stroked him. "Chris is a bit odd, isn't she?"

Odd or not, she had to face her new flatmates.

She got something to eat from the kitchen and found Chris in the dining room with a cross stitch project and gave her a small wave.

Tom sat on the balcony floor. He'd hung a beach towel over the balcony railing, using it as a shield to stay hidden from anyone in the street below. A book lay open on his lap, an unopened chocolate bar on top of it.

The air was mild. Puffy clouds littered the sky.

Anna stood in the balcony doorway and bit into one of Chris' oatmeal bars. The taste of dried fruit filled her mouth and she wrinkled her nose. "Yuck. Raisins."

Tom's shoulders shook as he chuckled into his book. "I don't like them either."

Anna politely broke off the piece she'd bitten into and put the rest of the bar back into the Tupperware container. She glanced apologetically at Chris who was sitting at the dining room table, her eyes narrowed as she focused on her needlework. "These are definitely not for me." Anna grinned and sheepishly added, "Sorry."

Chris looked up and smiled. "Don't apologise. More for me. I can make the next batch with nuts if you prefer?"

"Thank you."

"There's a cup of gross lukewarm instant coffee next to the sink."

Anna grimaced, reached for the cup and took a sip, all the while giving her coffee machine a sad look. She missed *real* coffee.

She stepped back outside and sat down next to Tom. He didn't look up, his eyes red and glassy.

"Are you okay? Why aren't you sleeping?"

He didn't reply, but his eyes flicked between his mother and his book.

"What are you reading?"

"I'm not. I'm just watching the road in case someone else tries to break in."

"Oh. Did your mum tell you to do that?"

He shook his head. His bottom lip quivered, and he bit down on it. Once again, his eyes flicked to his mother. As if he were afraid. "I miss Dad."

"Tell me about him?"

"It's not just dad," Tom said. "Mum's been…" He fell silent. "She's done all these things…I asked her if we could go to James'. He's my best friend and his dad owns a farm, but Mum said we couldn't go because they might not have room for us."

Anna raised an eyebrow. Chris hadn't mentioned a farm and they'd only spoken about growing food the other day. "Where does James live?"

"Near Ware."

"Your mum is right. That's a bit far."

"You walked all the way to Colchester and back." Tom tore open the plastic wrapping and offered her the first bite of his chocolate bar.

Anna declined with a wave of her hand. "Enjoy."

"Ware is a lot closer than Colchester," Tom added before taking a bite.

"It's different because I'm an adult—"

Tom snorted. "I'm almost fourteen."

"Sarah's my sister. I had to try and find her."

He gave her a defiant look. "James is my best friend. We've known each other since we were little. How's that different?"

"You're right. It's not. I'll talk to your mum and ask if we can check on James once it's safe."

Anna watched Tom chew. He had pale green eyes with long dark lashes. In a few years, he'd have turned heads wherever he went, but now…what a pity.

Instead of enjoying girls and parties, he'd have to hide, fight and survive.

"How long had your dad been ill?"

"That's not what killed him…" Tom fell silent and rubbed his eyes. They were more bloodshot than when she'd got back. He looked like he hadn't slept in days, which only fuelled the growing worry gnawing at her.

Something had happened.

Being robbed at gunpoint would be traumatic for anyone, let alone a teenage boy, but nobody had been hurt. John had left. Could Tom still be upset over that? Or was there something more?

Anna's voice dropped to a whisper. "Did something happen between you and your mum while I was away? You look scared."

Tom shook his head and took another bite.

"Do you want to talk some more about what happened to your dad? It's hard to deal with a suicide. It's normal to feel sad and angry. It's normal not to sleep. You need to talk about it. It'll help."

"It wasn't suicide," he spat, his eyes flashing. "I know he was ill, but he was never that poorly. It's…it's my mum. She was…" He swallowed. "She was covered in his blood. I think she's dange—"

"What are you two muttering about?" Chris asked, interrupting her son, her tone sharp. Tom flinched as if he'd been struck and turned his attention back to his book. He stuffed the rest of the chocolate into his mouth. "Nothing," he mumbled.

Anna turned and looked up at Chris. Her mind whirled

with unanswered questions. Had Chris heard what her son had said?

"He's upset about his dad," Anna said.

Tom jumped to his feet, tossed the wrapper over the balcony railing and ran off, slamming the door to the spare room.

Anna frowned, staring at Chris. The woman was so skinny she appeared fragile, like a twig in danger of snapping. The hardness Anna had spotted in Chris' eyes seemed to have taken up permanent residence there.

"It's a tragedy, really." Chris sat down next to Anna. She was chewing on the inside of her cheek, her lips pursed. She looked more pensive than angry. Anna hoped she hadn't heard what Tom had said.

Could Chris be dangerous?

Anna thought of Bob's question: *How do you spot evil?*

The woman next to her didn't look like Anna would have imagined evil.

At all.

But it was always like that wasn't it? Whenever friends and neighbours were interviewed after someone had committed a particularly heinous crime, everyone came out and said, "But she was always so quiet and polite."

Her father was quiet and polite outside the home as well.

"I have one bottle of beer left," Anna said, trying to break the tension. "Fancy sharing it?"

Chris nodded.

She got up and opened the fridge. It felt weird opening the door and not being greeted by a bright light and cold air.

She exhaled slowly, rolling her shoulders. She hadn't realised just how tense Chris' presence made her.

"Anna?"

"Coming." She grabbed the bottle and opened it with the help of her keyring before handing it to Chris. "I'm sorry it's warm." She sat down again and leaned her back against the wall of her small balcony. "I found a note at Sarah's. She said to come back here and wait for her."

Anna didn't mention the secret meeting spot. She kept that to herself. Just in case.

The two women sat side by side on the balcony, the sun bathing their legs in a warm light.

Chris scratched behind her ear, peering at Anna through long lashes. "Where do you think she is?"

"I don't know."

The sound of three consecutive gunshots being fired pierced the silence, and Anna got to her feet to look over the railing. She leaned forward but couldn't see anything.

Was there trouble at Sainsbury's?

"I'm scared," Chris said.

Anna hesitated, giving Chris a long look. Was she really scared? Chris looked determined, her mouth hard. "The army hung looters from street signs in Braintree."

"Seriously?"

"Colchester is on fire. When I left, the smoke was so thick you could barely see your own hand."

Chris took a sip of beer before handing the bottle back to Anna. "I wonder if they're withdrawing to the town centre and abandoning the outskirts of Harlow. It doesn't make sense for them to waste army resources. I'd grab everything and build a fort somewhere."

Anna stared at the label on the bottle. "Do you think it's better for people to know we're here or not? If people see us, they'll think we have food, won't they? But people would be less likely to loot somewhere occupied, right?"

"We need guns."

Anna winced. "Do we?"

"How else are we going to defend ourselves against soldiers? They carry guns."

Anna took a sip and handed the bottle back to Chris. "It's weird, isn't it?"

"What do you mean?"

"How much life has changed in just two weeks. How everything we're used to has gone. How we'll never have another burger or milkshake. How there are no more books to buy, no museums to visit, no restaurants to eat in. It's bloody strange."

Chris chuckled. "You have enough books sitting on your shelves."

"Who would have thought that one day I'd be glad to have this many books stacked in my flat."

Chris handed the bottle back to Anna. "Have the rest."

"I'm scared of what comes next," Anna said, taking another sip of the lukewarm beer. She made a face and put the bottle down. "Did you end up going to Poundland?"

"We did but then…he took half, Anna. What are we going to do?"

Anna sighed. "I don't know. How long until we run out?"

"Two months without Sarah. Are you going to set out and look for her again?"

Anna frowned. Was Chris trying to get rid of her?

What if Sarah wasn't at Pet's Corner come morning? What if she had got lost? What if she was one of those bodies lying in a field somewhere?

"She could be anywhere. I don't even know where to start looking."

If for any reason your flat isn't safe, meet me at sunrise where Mum used to take us every Sunday morning.

Was her flat safe? Anna's thoughts drifted to Tom's sunken eyes. *I think she's dangerous.*

Had Sarah shown up while Anna had been away? Would Chris really lie to her?

Or had Sarah seen Tom on the balcony and decided to stay away?

Anna didn't know anything about Chris, except that her husband had been depressed. Was she even a nurse? Was there any way she could check?

Walk over to the hospital and ask?

If Sarah wasn't at Pet's Corner come morning, Anna wouldn't know what to do next. She had no plan. Nobody to turn to.

Without Sarah, she felt alone. A growing sense of dread sent a shiver down her back.

Perhaps she could ask Tom what he'd meant when he said that Chris was dangerous.

"I'll take the watch tonight," Anna said after a long silence. If she wanted to go to Pet's Corner, she needed to leave the house in the early hours of the morning.

Chris nodded and yawned.

Anna needed to be alone with Tom. Perhaps she could help him teach Oreo a few tricks.

Oreo! That was it! Her chance to discover the truth. "I think Oreo needs to go outside. Would you mind taking him? My knee's still in a lot of pain."

Chris struggled to her feet. "Of course."

Anna waited for the front door to close before getting up. She took some of Oreo's treats, knocked on the door to the spare room and poked her head inside. "Tom? Here's some treats you can give to Oreo later. You two seem to be getting along."

He looked up and grinned for the first time since their arrival. "Thank you."

Anna took a deep breath. She had five minutes at most before Chris would be back. "I want to ask you something, and I need you to be honest with me."

He pressed his lips together, his eyes hardening.

"Did my sister come here?"

He shook his head but didn't meet her eyes.

"Tom? Please tell me the truth." Anna fell silent, waiting for him to look up again. When he didn't, she whispered, "What did you mean before when you said that your mum was dangerous?"

She heard the front door open and close. Tom winced.

"Is there a problem?" Chris asked, unclipping Oreo's lead.

Anna closed the door to the spare room. "I was just giving Tom some treats for Oreo. They get along so well." She could barely keep her voice from shaking.

What had Tom meant when he'd said that his dad hadn't committed suicide?

Unease made her skin crawl, and she rubbed her lower arm where goosebumps had formed.

15

Anna paced back and forth in her bedroom, walking over the small rug in front of her bed, forcing herself to turn every few steps, but she didn't dare risk waking Chris. Every few minutes she stopped and listened to the soft snores coming from the spare room.

Moonlight shone through the blinds. Soon, she'd have to set out for Pet's Corner.

What if Chris didn't let her back in?

Anna curled her toes into the rug.

What if Sarah *had* come here, and Chris had turned her away?

What if they'd fought?

What if Chris had...hurt Sarah?

Anna ran her hands through her hair. For the first time since she'd moved out of her childhood home, she allowed the voice in her mind to resurface. To scare her.

What if...

She'd tried not to listen to it when it had first piped up, but it was growing stronger.

Chris had admitted to poisoning the food she'd given to

John. She was proactive and determined; she wouldn't let anything come between her and survival.

I think she's dangerous.

The hair on her neck stood on end at the memory of Tom's words. Anna rubbed her bare arms. If only Tom had been willing to talk to her. Perhaps if she had more time alone with him? But how? It wasn't like she could send Chris out to buy milk and tea bags.

Soft, quiet steps pulled her from her thoughts. The door to her room opened. Anna recognised Tom's silhouette in the dark.

Oreo jumped off her bed to greet him. Tom bent down to stroke the dog before slipping a folded piece of paper into Anna's hands.

"Wha—"

He shook his head, pressing his index finger against his lips before tiptoeing back out of the room.

Anna lit a candle on her bedside table with a match and sat down on her bed. She unfolded the paper and angled it so she could read it.

He'd torn it from a notebook.

She narrowed her eyes, trying to decipher Tom's scraggly handwriting.

Somebody knocked on the door the day after the soldier had robbed us. A woman asked for you. I think it was Sarah. Mum didn't want to open the door, but when the woman wouldn't stop knocking, she went outside. I heard shouting, then it sounded as if somebody was falling down the stairs. Mum came back half an hour later and when I asked what had happened, she brushed me off.

He'd written another line below then crossed it out. She held the note closer to the candle but couldn't make out the words.

The note continued: *The night of the EMP, I went looking*

for her and her boss threatened me. Mum killed him. Just like that. She claims that Dad was dead when she found him, but she was covered in his blood. She won't talk about it.

Please burn this. Please don't tell her I said anything.

Anna's heart thudded so loudly in her chest she worried it might wake Chris in the other room. Ragged breathing threatened to turn into a full-blown panic attack. She pressed her hand against her mouth, stifling her sobs.

Sarah had been here.

Chris had hurt her.

Had her sister managed to get away?

Anna opened her window and used the candle to burn the note in her hand. The paper shrivelled up as the flames consumed Tom's handwriting. She blew on the remains until there was nothing but smoke and tossed the ashes into the wind.

She opened her wardrobe and found loose jogging trousers before shuffling into the kitchen, still carrying the candle.

She inspected her arsenal of potential weapons: rat poison, steak knives and a can of pepper spray.

Chris had the other can.

Anna's eyes wandered over her spice rack. If necessary, she could create a makeshift acid with chilli powder. Anna held onto the kitchen counter, unmoving.

Paralysed.

Her hands gripped the edges, the blood draining from her knuckles. She fought down a surge of panic. Sucking on her bottom lip, she tried to keep the voice in her head from overwhelming her.

Don't ever hesitate, Chris. Act.

She'd said those words to Chris, and now the woman was heeding her advice.

Anna shoved the can of pepper spray into her trouser pocket.

She had to search the other flats. Make sure Chris hadn't dumped Sarah's body somewhere. Anna waited in the kitchen until daylight trickled in through the window.

Sarah *had* been here.

What if she was tied up and gagged in one of the flats below?

You're being drama—

No.

Chris had been willing to kill. More than once.

Anna pushed the chest of drawers out of the way and opened the front door, inspecting the stairwell for blood. On her hands and knees, she searched the cold surface, looking for any change in colour or residue.

The steps smelled of bleach.

She went down one flight of stairs to the third-floor landing. She noticed a dark spot by the front door to the flat there. It looked like somebody had scrubbed the concrete, but that spot could have been there before. It wasn't as if the staircase had been clean to begin with.

Her knee twinged as she struggled back to her feet.

If Chris had killed Sarah, she would have had to dispose of the body. But where?

She knocked on the door. Oreo trotted down the stairs. He tilted his head, his black eyes watching her.

She tried to open the door, but it was locked. The couple living there spent a lot of time abroad. She hadn't seen them in weeks.

"Wait for me," she said to Oreo, then walked down another flight of stairs and entered the flat on the second floor. It looked just like she'd left it after splitting everything inside with her neighbours on the ground floor. The cupboards and drawers were still open. A thin layer of dust covered the kitchen table.

The flat on the first floor was still locked. The previous tenants had moved out a couple of months ago. The letting agency had the keys.

Anna knew the ground-floor flat was occupied—she'd heard their toddler scream more than once since the EMP—and decided to head outside first. She inspected the communal patch of grass at the back of the block. It was thriving in the English summer rain.

Uncut. Untouched.

Anna went back inside and knocked on the door of the ground-floor flat. The young father opened it with the door chain firmly slotted in.

"Hello," Anna stammered, her cheeks growing hot. "We've met before. I live—"

"Top floor, I know." He narrowed his eyes. "Anna, right?"

"Uhm…" She pinched the bridge of her nose. "I'm looking for my sister. She was supposed to come here…she's a lot taller, but we look pretty much alike."

He shook his head. "I've only seen that other woman with her son."

"Did you hear anything the last few nights? Fighting? Shouting?"

"No, sorry." He scratched his beard, his cheeks blotchy.

"Are you all right?"

"Maddie's sick. The hospital sent us home with antibiotics." He yawned. "Any news on the power coming back on? Or when the next supply crate is due? We're almost out of water."

Anna frowned. "The power coming back on?"

"Yes? I didn't think it would take them two weeks. I'm sure I heard gunshots earlier today. They were busy at the hospital as well."

Anna blinked. Did he really think the power would be back? And that the government would continue supplying food and water?

"No, I haven't heard any news, sorry." Anna swallowed and wondered if she should tell him more, but she didn't want another person knowing about the food in her flat.

He smiled. "Give us a shout if you need anything."

Baffled, Anna nodded. "Likewise."

"I hope you find your sister." He closed the door.

"Anna? What are you doing?" Chris' voice travelled through the stairwell.

Anna headed back upstairs, gathering her courage. Oreo was waiting on the third floor. She gestured for him to go upstairs. "I was just…" She gave a small shrug and closed the door to her apartment, then pushed the chest of drawers back in front of it.

She followed Chris into the kitchen and watched as the woman warmed a mug of water over three candles before mixing coffee into it.

Tears stung Anna's eyes. She'd been so scared that she would find Sarah's body that she'd forgotten to go to Pet's Corner.

She couldn't let fear overwhelm her.

Not if she wanted to survive.

Anna took a deep breath. "Be honest with me, Chris. Did anyone else knock? Was anyone else here?"

"Why do you keep asking?" Chris snapped.

Behind her, Tom shook his head, eyes widening in horror, but Anna ignored him. She wrapped her hand around the pepper spray in her trousers. "Because my sister is missing!" Tears of frustration blurred her vision and she bit back a curse. "She said she'd come here, and I need to know what you've done to her."

Chris blinked. "Why would I have done something to her? Where is this coming from?"

"You killed your manager."

Chris whirled around and glared at her son. "Did you tell her that? Are you the one filling her head with these silly ideas?"

"No, Mum—"

"Yes, I stabbed Mike." Chris turned back to Anna. "And I'm not sorry that he's dead, but you can't listen to Tom. He's traumatised. He's thirteen. He doesn't understand these things." Her face grew increasingly red as she spoke. "Mike threatened Tom with his taser. You saw him do that to us, Anna. Yes, I killed him, but what else was I supposed to do?"

Anna leaned against the fridge to hide her trembling hands. "He threatened Tom with *his taser*?" She looked at Tom. "Is that true?"

He nodded.

"Couldn't you have knocked him out or something?"

Chris bristled with anger. "He aimed his taser at me and fired. I guess the EMP had damaged it and it didn't work. I stabbed him. I did it to save my son. Like you said Anna, the time to be polite is over. We need to act. And I did. I kept us safe."

Anna frowned. "What about John? The soldier? Did you have to poison him?"

Chris raised both eyebrows. "Seriously? He was robbing us, Anna. He was going to come back. I was protecting *your* flat. *Your* food."

"And that's when you realised that the remaining food wouldn't be enough for the four of us." Spittle flew from Anna's mouth and she wiped her chin with the back of her hand. "What have you done to my sister?"

"Nothing, Anna. Sarah didn't come knocking. Somebody did, yes." She gave her son a long look. "That woman claimed to be your sister, but she didn't match the description you'd given me. I threatened her. She left."

"Oh?" Anna scowled. This story made no sense. Why would anyone come to her flat and pretend to be her sister? "What did she look like?"

"Skinny with dark, curly hair. It doesn't matter, Anna." Chris tucked a strand of hair behind her ear and grimaced. "You won't believe me either way."

Chris was right. Anna didn't believe her. "What about your husband?"

Chris paled. "What about him?"

"You were in the room with him when he—"

"No." Chris' eyes bulged. "He was dead when I found him. I sat there for hours. I didn't hurt him. His skin was so cold…he must have died before my shift ended." She turned to Tom. "You have to believe me. I'd have never hurt your dad."

Anna scoffed. *I told him…I told him we'd be better off without him.* "That's not true, you—" She stopped, seeing the hatred flash in Chris' eyes.

But it was too late. Tom took a step towards Chris. "What did you do, Mum?"

"Nothing," Chris said quickly.

"Mum?"

Anna thought back to Chris' words: *If Tom ever finds out what I said…if he finds out that I'm the reason his father is dead, he'll never speak to me again.*

She thought of the despair clouding Chris' eyes. That hadn't been a lie.

"Your mum told me that she'd been fighting a lot with your dad." Deflated, Anna sank to the floor. "I don't know what to do, Chris. I don't trust you. And I don't know how to believe that you're telling the truth."

"I know," Chris said softly. "I'm sorry."

16

ANNA RETREATED TO HER BEDROOM AND CLOSED THE DOOR. She pressed her face into a pillow and screamed. Tears soaked into the fabric. Oreo nudged her with his nose, and her hand found his soft fur.

Fear and confusion overwhelmed her, her stomach knotting with pain from the stress. She dropped the pillow and glanced outside where the sun illuminated the trees lining the edges of the park.

Pet's Corner was only fifteen minutes away.

Hopefully, her sister would be there the next morning, waiting for her, annoyed she'd taken so long.

But what if she wasn't there? What if Sarah had given up? Or was hurt somewhere between Colchester and Harlow?

And what if Chris didn't let Anna back in afterwards? Where would she go?

Unable to contain the nagging voice in her head any longer, Anna sobbed into the pillow. The voice wouldn't let up. Wouldn't be silenced.

She'd be without food and water. Without medicine.

Unless…

Unless she packed a bag. Unless she was ready to leave

the flat behind.

For the third time in two weeks, Anna was faced with a potentially life-changing choice.

She either believed Chris' words, believed that she had not met Sarah and assumed Chris was an ally—someone she could trust—and waited near Pet's Corner every morning at sunrise. Or she—

Anna pressed her knuckles into her temples and groaned.

Did she really have a choice? The dog opened one eye and gave her a concerned look.

She didn't doubt that Chris had told her the truth about Mike. The man had been a threat, and the memory of his derisive sneer sent a shiver down her spine. If it hadn't been for the security guard, they'd have been in trouble.

It wasn't as if Chris could have called the police, and she'd been alone with her son, late at night with no one there to help.

Anna would have done the same, but she couldn't deny the hardness around Chris' mouth. The determination lifting her chin. Or the darkness within her eyes.

And what if Anna got in Chris' way? Now Chris had access to the flat and supplies, Anna had outlived her usefulness. She was just another mouth to feed. Another mouth endangering Tom's survival.

How long would it take for Chris to show her true colours?

According to Tom's note, it *had* been Sarah who'd knocked. Who else would have known about Sarah? Could it have been one of Anna's colleagues?

Anna didn't think anybody knew where she lived.

Or that she had a sister.

Apart from her dad.

Skinny. Dark, curly hair. She knew nobody who matched that description.

Lester was another story entirely. Why would Chris hurt her own husband? His father's death must have traumatised Tom. It was tough to lose a parent. Even tougher in a situation like this.

Perhaps the boy was imagining things?

Anna couldn't imagine having to face the end of the world as they knew it while battling something as cruel as depression. She found it hard enough to get up in the mornings as it was.

On the other hand, Chris had proved her willingness to kill for her son. Kill to ensure her own survival.

It didn't matter if Tom's account had been true. Anna couldn't trust Chris.

Not after everything that had happened.

Not now she knew about Mike. And about the young soldier. He'd looked barely eighteen. Threat or not, Chris hadn't cared that he would be taking food—poisoned food—home to his family. To his baby.

Anna had to act before it was too late. Her mind drifted back to Bob's words: *Do you think it's possible to spot evil?*

At the very least Chris was ruthless.

Anna wouldn't make it on her own, but how could she ever trust another person?

One day at a time.

Firstly, she had to deal with Chris.

Anna didn't want to give up her own flat and leave, but Chris was the kind of woman who'd come back if shown the door. Back to take what wasn't hers.

At least if Anna were to leave, Chris wouldn't know where to find her, wouldn't have a reason to chase her, and Anna wouldn't have to constantly look over her shoulder.

Chris would cease being a danger.

Anna gently pulled on a matted bit of fur behind Oreo's ear and he playfully hit her chest with his paw. She tickled his feet and he pulled away. "What would you do?" she asked, and the dog yawned in reply.

"Chris, I'm sorry but I can't trust you and you have to leave." Anna savoured each word, her stomach constricting at the thought of facing Chris.

She'd never sleep soundly again. Always having to look over her shoulder. Always waiting for Chris to return.

Anna sighed and patted Oreo's back. "Looks like we're the ones who have to leave."

Or...

The voice in her mind piped up, and Anna squeezed her eyes shut.

Or...

Anna winced.

Or...

She didn't want to face the thought buried in the dark recesses of her mind. Didn't want to invite it to come closer. It hovered just outside of her reach, and Anna pressed her knuckles into her eyes.

Or...

It was the only way for her to keep her flat *and* feel safe.

She had to—

She had to kill Chris.

Anna jumped to her feet, and Oreo flinched at the sudden movement. He scratched a spot behind his ear and yawned again.

Anna curled her toes into the soft rug in front of her bed.

No! You're being unfair.

Chris had done absolutely nothing to deserve Anna's suspicions.

Not only had the poor woman been forced to protect her son against a dangerous individual, but her husband had committed suicide, leaving her alone with her teenage son in a time of need.

Chris had brought food and water with her and asked for a place to stay. She'd protected the flat, talked John out of taking everything from them and made sure he wouldn't come back.

She'd risked her life to get them more food from the Poundland warehouse.

Chris had never even mentioned Anna's neighbours—hadn't shown the slightest interest in them. She hadn't suggested stealing supplies from others.

Instead, she'd spoken of finding a community. Growing food. Working together.

How could Anna think of killing—*murdering*—her?

"We'll go to Pet's Corner early tomorrow. Just the two of us." She scratched behind Oreo's ear and he gave her a long look as if questioning her logic. "Chris isn't our enemy. Don't worry. She'll let us back in."

Oreo whined in reply.

"Or maybe she won't."

She had to kill Chris.

A wave of nausea washed over her, and she put her hand over her mouth, swallowing the taste of bile. She was condemning a woman—a mother—to death because of her own fears.

What about Tom?

He was just a child. Only thirteen years old. Scared of his own mother. He'd given her a pleading look with red-rimmed eyes and told her to burn the note. He'd called his mother dangerous and implied that she'd killed his father.

Anna groaned. "Oh, Sarah. Where are you? I need your help."

She couldn't find Sarah without leaving her flat, and if she left her flat Chris could barricade the door.

She had to kill Chris.

Only then would she feel safe.

Perhaps Tom could help. Could she trust hi—

Of course not.

Anna buried her face in her hands. What was she thinking?

Chris was his mum. He'd stand by her. And Anna couldn't *murder* a child.

She flinched as if physically pained by the thoughts circling around in her mind.

No. *She* had to leave the flat. Find someplace else to make a home. She wasn't a murderer. She'd never even hit anyone. If she stayed, she'd never be safe, and she wasn't willing to go that far to survive.

Or was she?

It's your flat! Your food! Not hers.

What was she going to do? Where was she going to go? And what if Sarah wasn't at Pet's Corner?

Chris had knifed her manager, had crumbled rat poison into the food John had taken.

Anna froze.

The rat poison.

It would be ironic.

She had to make a decision before it was too late.

"What if I'm wrong?"

Oreo rolled onto his back and stretched. Anna patted his belly.

If she was wrong, an innocent woman would die.

Better her than you.

Like Bob had said: *We need to survive. And what we have to do in order to survive has changed since the EMP.*

Anna opened the bedroom door, tilted her head and listened. The flat was quiet. She shuffled into the kitchen and leaned against the counter, her heart pounding in her ears.

"Good morning, Anna," Tom said with a cheerful smile plastered across his face as if trying to defuse the tension before it could build. He sat next to Chris who was reading one of Anna's many crime thrillers, her bare feet resting on a chair.

Chris didn't look up. Her eyes were red and swollen. She looked like she'd been crying.

Anna swallowed.

What if I'm wrong?

"Morning," Anna replied.

"May I take your laptop apart?"

"My laptop?"

"I'm trying to figure out why some electronics have survived the EMP while others are toast."

Anna thought of all the photos of her mum and sister she had on there. "I—" She scratched her temple. It took everything she had to calmly lean against the kitchen counter. Her mind was screaming at her to get out. She swallowed and tried to keep her voice from shaking. "Can you save my photos?"

"I can remove the hard drive," Tom said. "I can't access it without a working laptop, but who knows…"

"Sure. Go ahead." Anna shook an almost empty Tupperware container. "I'm going to make new oatmeal bars for us."

The time to act had come.

Goosebumps covered her arms, and she rubbed her hands together. Anna stuck her head into the dining room, waiting for Chris to meet her eyes. "Dried fruit for you, right? I'll make mine with nuts instead."

Chris shrugged. "That's kind of you, but I can make my own later."

Anna forced a smile. "No worries. It's no trouble to make them all at the same time." Anna rolled up her sleeves and got out two bowls from the cupboard above her stove. "Tom? Do you want nuts in yours or something else?"

"Nuts, please."

Making sure she wasn't visible where she stood, Anna retrieved the box of rat poison from the cupboard underneath her sink and crumbled it into the bowl with oats. She whistled to distract herself, drizzling honey into the mixture with trembling hands.

"Do you need help?"

Anna's heart was in her throat as she turned around.

It was Chris.

"No. I'm fine." She forced a thin-lipped smile, hiding the rat poison with her body.

Chris smiled but the smile didn't reach her eyes. "I'm sorry…about everything. I'm—"

"It's okay," Anna said, the blood rushing in her ears as she held onto the kitchen counter with one hand.

"Are you sure you're all right?"

Anna nodded, not trusting her voice not to shake.

What if I'm wrong?

Chris left the kitchen, and Anna breathed a sigh of relief. She quickly placed the box back into the cupboard.

Almost.

She spread the mixture on an oiled tray and flattened it with a spatula before setting it aside so it could set.

Tom was tinkering with her laptop.

She had to make sure he wouldn't touch the poisoned food. "This slab is made with dried fruit," Anna said, and he laughed.

"Thank you for the warning."

She needed to stay calm. To focus.

She couldn't let fear overwhelm her.

Without her fridge, it would take a few hours for the mixture to set. She'd cut it into bars and give them all to Chris. She'd promise to trust her again.

And then she'd wait.

Taking a deep breath, Anna set out to prepare a second batch with nuts for herself and Tom.

IT WAS late in the afternoon and the sky was beginning to change colour to a darker blue when Tom entered the kitchen. Anna was cleaning.

"I was just wondering if—" His eyes fell onto the open cupboard where the box of rat poison sat on the uppermost shelf. He paled. "Why is that box open?"

"What box?"

"The rat poison. Mum put it away after…after that soldier…what are you doing?"

Anna swallowed. He was just a child. She couldn't do this to him.

What have I done!

She resisted the urge to run to Chris, grab the Tupperware and throw it into the bin.

It's too late.

She had to remain calm.

Trust your instinct. You can do this.

"Anna. You can't…" Tom's voice cracked. "You want us to go? We'll go. I have an uncle in Waltham Abbey. I can take her there, but please don't hurt her."

"I don't know what else to do," Anna whispered. "What if she comes back? How can I ever feel safe? You said yourself that she's dangerous."

"I'll make sure she doesn't come back. Please." Tom darted forward and grabbed the rat poison.

Anna held him by his elbow, but he pulled back. Poison pellets spilled over the counter. "Tom—"

"What is going on in here?" Chris's voice cut through the

tension in the air, and her eyes flicked from the box to her son's face and back to the box.

Rage transformed her features into an ugly grimace.

Anna took a step back, retrieved the pepper spray from her pocket and unloaded the can in Chris' face.

Tears poured down Chris' cheeks and she shrieked, one arm across her eyes, the other blindly reaching for Anna.

Anna shoved Chris away. "Get out of my home."

Chris' nails scratched Anna's hands and face as she grabbed her hair, pulling hard. Anna staggered, and Chris wrapped her arms around her waist, locking her in an iron grip. "Tom."

Tom stood frozen in place. His eyes widened with panic.

Anna forcefully kicked Chris in the shin, but the woman didn't let go. She was trapped. Chris was stronger than her. Tom was her only chance. "Tom! She told your dad that she wished he would—"

Chris let go and screamed, throwing her entire weight at Anna. Anna swiftly stepped to the side and Chris hurtled into the kitchen door. The cheap wood splintered, and Anna grabbed Chris's shoulders, wrestling her to the ground. Her anger spiked, and she dug her knee into Chris' chest, pressing her head into the floor with her hand.

Chris wheezed. "Tom!"

Anna gasped for air. "Stop struggling."

"I'm sorry," Tom whispered. Strong hands wrapped around Anna's neck from behind.

The edges of her vision blurred. Anna flailed and kicked, her foot connecting with something hard, but Tom's grip tightened.

She gasped for air.

Oreo barked, but Anna knew he wouldn't bite.

Her world went dark.

17

A HIGH-PITCHED RINGING SOUND CUT THROUGH HER PEACEFUL dreams. Anna winced, her head pounding. Blood rushing in her ears. She opened one eye and bright daylight blinded her.

Unable to orientate herself, she groaned. Her throat ached as if—

Somebody had tried strangling her. "Wh—"

She couldn't move her tongue. Saliva trickled from her mouth down her chin. She tried to wipe her mouth, but her limbs wouldn't obey. Her head felt like it had doubled in size. Pulsating. Buzzing. Pounding behind her right eye.

Where am I?

She blinked. Focused.

Her dining room. She was sitting—

She was tied to a chair.

Something sharp dug into her wrists. The flesh rubbed raw. Burning.

Anna opened her mouth again and almost choked on fabric. A tea towel?

Somebody had gagged her.

She wiggled her hands, but the bonds were too tight. The more she moved, the deeper they dug into her wrists. She tried to stand, but they'd bound her ankles too. Her skin burned as if on fire.

Chris' voice cut through the haze. "You're finally awake."

Anna frowned, narrowing her eyes.

"My son begged me not to kill you." Chris stood in the doorway to the kitchen holding Anna's biggest knife in her hand. The only weapon in her flat, save for the last can of pepper spray.

Chris came into focus as she stepped into the dining room. A black bruise had formed under her eye from where she'd slammed into the kitchen door. It was still spreading. The expression on her face morphed from serious to menacing as she moved towards Anna.

Towering above her, Chris held the carving knife to Anna's throat.

Anna gagged. Coughed. Unable to breathe, panic flooded her.

She's going to kill me.

Chris removed the gag from Anna's mouth and took a step back.

"Where's—" Anna coughed. Spat. "Where's Oreo?"

"In your bedroom." Chris smiled. It distorted her face. Perhaps she thought it made her look kinder, but it was an ugly smile. "I would never hurt your dog, but I was worried he might try and bite. You never know, seeing you tied up like that."

Anna stared at Chris. The edges of her vision were still blurred as the headache continued to build behind her right eye. She had nothing to lose. "Did you kill my sister?" She struggled not to slur the words, and her stomach twisted at the thought.

"No," Chris said. "I didn't. She left. After a brief...struggle."

I wasn't wrong. Sarah was here.

Relief washed over Anna. She'd poisoned—

Fog filled her mind, distorting her memories.

Focus.

She'd poisoned the oatmeal bars. She'd put the Tupperware container down next to Chris. Had smiled. Apologised. Had waited for her to take a bar before hiding in her room.

She hadn't wanted to watch.

How long would it take for the poison to take effect? How much would she have to eat for it to work?

Chris drifted in and out of focus and Anna felt nauseous. What if Chris died while she was tied to this chair?

Would Tom help her? Or would he walk away and leave her to starve?

A whimper escaped Anna's mouth. "Sarah left? Did she say where she was going?"

"I didn't ask." Chris shrugged. "I told her that you'd gone to Colchester and that you'd left the flat to me. It took a while, but she finally believed me."

Anna's gaze drifted to Tom. He stood next to his mother with his hands jammed into his trouser pockets. "Tom? Why did you…"

Tom didn't reply, couldn't meet her eyes.

"Did you really think you could turn my own son against me?" Chris placed a hand on her hip, pursing her lips. "The position you put me in, Anna…why would you do that? Now I have to kill you. You've left me no choice."

Tom gasped. "Mum! You promised you wouldn't hurt her!"

Chris ignored him. "If I throw you out, you might bring your mates or a few soldiers. Try and take back what you think is yours. I'm not prepared to risk my son's life. Not after you planned to poison me."

"I wouldn't—"

"You planned on killing me, Anna. You pretended to be

kind and welcoming. You pretended to be my friend." She scoffed. "I couldn't believe my eyes when I saw the open box of poison. Who would do something like that?"

Tom's eyes swam with tears.

You planned to poison me. Chris didn't know it had already happened. She didn't know the oatmeal bars had been—

"You're upsetting your son," Anna whispered.

Chris' stare hardened. "How *dare* you talk about my son. You were going to murder me—his mother. How sick is that?"

"I had to—"

"You had to?"

Anna swallowed. She'd had to, hadn't she? "You're scared of me? I'm terrified of you. I didn't feel safe in my own home. Even Tom thinks you killed his—"

"I did *not*." Fury flashed in her eyes. "I didn't hurt Lester."

"You admitted to poisoning Jo—"

"To protect us!"

Anna lifted her chin defiantly. "To protect *yourself* and your *son*. You've proved your willingness to kill anyone standing in your way. What if that's me one day? Do I just wait? What would you have done in my situation, Chris?"

"*You* told me to act," Chris said softly.

"I told you to act, and that's what I did as well. I want to survive, Chris."

Chris raised the knife. "Don't we all?"

Anna flinched. She had to buy herself time.

Somehow.

Until the poison began to work.

She cried, "Please don't kill me." Thoughts were swirling around her head. She needed more time. Perhaps if she apologised? Begged? Asked Chris to untie her so she could stroke Oreo one last time?

"You've left me no choice," Chris repeated.

"Mum?"

"I'm sorry, Tom, but she's dangerous. You have to trust me."

Anna sniffled. "If I could just—"

"Shut up," Chris barked.

Tom sobbed. "Mum—"

The blade of the carving knife sparkled in the pale sunlight. "Everyone shut up. Now. I need to think."

Anna closed her eyes, tears falling down her cheeks. She bit her lip and waited.

Let it be quick. Please let it be quick.

A knife to the throat had to be better than being burned alive or shot in the back by a rogue soldier. Her breathing quickened as she braced herself for the cold steel against her skin.

A faint sound caught her attention. She tilted her head and listened. Oreo's paws scampered across her bedroom floor.

She knew that sound. He was spinning around.

Somebody was in the stairwell and Oreo knew whoever it was.

It had to be Sarah.

Adrenaline spiked in her stomach. She had to distract Chris. She had to make sure the woman wouldn't notice the noise. "I'm truly sorry," she said loudly.

Tom cocked his head. Anna stiffened. Had he noticed Oreo moving about?

She had to distract them both.

CHRIS TIGHTENED her grip on the carving knife to keep it from shaking in her hand. The pounding of her heart was seemingly the only sound in the flat. Considering her options, she watched the blood drain from her knuckles.

How had this gone so wrong? What was she doing? The woman in front of her had been nothing but kind to her. Both Mike and John had been attacking her son. Attacking her. Weapon in hand.

It was kill or be killed.

But this was different. Anna was afraid. Tied to a chair.

Could Chris do this? Could she do what needed to be done?

This woman in front of her had planned to kill her.

Anna struggled, pulling on her ties, rocking the chair back and forth. Tom sat down at the dining table and buried his head in his hands.

Anna had turned out to be a lot stronger than she looked, and Chris had needed Tom's help to knock her out. But he'd stood motionless at first. Had watched Anna wrestle Chris to the ground. Had watched her knee digging into Chris' chest.

He'd only come to her aid at the last second.

Had he been afraid? Or had he briefly considered helping Anna?

No. Tom was her son. She could trust him.

What was she going to do now?

Anna was at her mercy.

And she had no other option but to kill her.

She didn't want to. She didn't want to give her son another reason to hate her. *You promised not to kill her.* She felt a pang of guilt thinking of Tom's words. The look he'd given her. As if she was a monster.

You are a monster.

Was she?

Chris bit back a sob.

If she let Anna go, they'd have no place to stay. They'd have to leave and—

There was no more food left. The soldiers packing the crates at the warehouse had all but admitted that the government had run out of supplies. Then John had confirmed it.

If she and Tom left Anna's flat, they'd have nothing. She wasn't going to give up their meagre supplies. She'd fought so hard for them. Had killed John and got rid of Sarah for them.

Anna was the only thing standing between them and survival.

Tom gave her a pleading look. "Mum? Can't we move into one of the downstairs flats?"

"Oh, sweetie…" Chris' voice trailed off as she studied Anna's face. It wasn't about the space. This flat. Their old home. None of it mattered.

What mattered were their supplies.

And that she could keep Tom safe.

Anna's eyes lit up at Tom's suggestion, but Chris shook her head. "I wish we could, but we've both admitted to not trusting each other. Anna was prepared to poison us. How could we ever live in the same building and feel safe?" She placed a hand on his shoulder. "Remember how I told you I'd have to make some tough decisions in the coming weeks? And that I need you to trust me?"

Tom nodded.

I'm sorry, but Anna has left. Sarah's gaze had stared right into her soul as if she were seeking the truth within Chris. She'd craned her neck, trying to peer past her and into the flat.

Perhaps she *was* a monster.

But after John had taken half the food, she hadn't seen any other way. She wiped her brow with the back of her hand.

If surviving meant turning into a monster, then that was what she'd do.

Her chest tightened. She'd never wished for anything like this to happen.

You enjoy—

No.

She didn't.

The cat. Its bulging eyes. The surge of power coursing through her veins as her knife had slid into Mike's stomach.

You enjoy this.

"No." Chris lowered the knife. It shook in her grip.

"Excuse me?" Anna frowned.

"I didn't mean for this to happen."

It was the truth. She hadn't. She'd planned on hiding, waiting for the end of this ordeal. Once the worst was over, she'd hoped to find a community. She was a nurse. She helped people. That was her job. She'd be an asset to any group of survivors.

Chris took a deep breath. "I didn't come here to hurt you, Anna. I came here because you'd helped me, and I was looking for a safe place for myself and my son.

"I know," Anna said.

"Do you understand why I'm doing this?" she asked Tom.

He sniffled, then whispered, "No."

He wouldn't forgive her, but as a mother she sometimes had to make tough choices and she could only hope that one day he would understand.

"One day you will." Chris raised the knife.

18

The rhythm of Oreo's feet pattering across the floor in her bedroom grew more frantic and Anna winced. She couldn't make him stop, not without saying anything.

If the person in the stairwell were a stranger, he'd be growling. Barking. Snarling. It had to be Sarah. She was the only other person whose steps he recognised.

"What's that noise?" Chris frowned and turned towards the bedroom.

Anna stiffened. She had to distract Chris before she connected the dots. Before she realised what Oreo was doing and why. Anna rocked sideways, moaning as if in pain and hoping the noise would mask Oreo's growing excitement to give Sarah enough time to slip into the flat unnoticed.

Her sister had a spare key, but she'd have to push hard against the door to move the chest of drawers out of the way.

The chair wobbled, leaning precariously to one side.

Chris scowled. "What are you doing?"

Frantic, Anna rocked back and forth again. The chair swayed, then tipped and clattered to the floor. Pain exploded in her right temple and the world went dark for a brief moment. She whimpered.

Oreo barked—most likely scared by the commotion—the sound muffled by the closed bedroom door.

The front door creaked.

Please be Sarah. Please be Sarah.

Anna turned her head. Blood trickled down her forehead and she squinted. *Noise. Make a noise.* She moaned. A dull ache radiated from her temple.

Tom rushed to her side and his knees thudded against the floor next to Anna's ear. "Mum. She's bleeding." He bent over her and gingerly touched her head. "She can't hurt us. You have to help her."

Chris took a step closer but didn't bother to bend down. "Don't worry. Head wounds look a lot scarier than they are."

Anna blinked. Blood blurred her vision.

Now what? She was on the floor, heartbeat pounding in her ears. Where was Sarah? Chris cocked her head as if focusing on something specific. Anna wet her lips, gathering the energy to scream.

Crack!

Above her, Chris' eyes suddenly widened. The small woman staggered and lost her balance. A groan escaped Chris' lips as she dropped to her knees. She opened her mouth as if to speak, then collapsed sideways, her eyes rolling back into her head.

Behind her, Sarah was holding a pistol as if it were a baseball bat instead of a firearm, her eyes fierce.

Tom looked up and gasped. "Mum?"

Relief washed over Anna and she sobbed. Tom crawled over to his unconscious mother. "Mum?" He pushed on her shoulders, rolling her over so she lay on her side.

"Don't move," Sarah barked, aiming her weapon at the boy. "Anna? Anna! Are you all right? You're bleeding."

"I'm fine." Anna hiccupped and laughed. "I'm fine. I'm so glad to see you."

Tom stared at the pistol, frozen to the spot.

Sarah's features softened, but she kept the gun aimed at his head. "Untie her."

Tom turned and shakily fiddled with the cable ties. Anna felt him tremble. "I need…" He swallowed. "I need scissors."

"It's okay, Tom," Anna said. "It's okay. Breathe. Look, your mum has dropped the knife. Why don't you use that?" She looked at her sister. "He's okay. Just scared." She didn't think he'd hurt her, but he could easily cut her wrists instead of the cable ties and Sarah wouldn't be able to stop him before it was too late.

She closed her eyes as Tom retrieved the knife and cut her ties.

"Thank you. Check on your mum," Anna said, sitting up. She turned to Sarah. "How did you know I was here?"

"That woman told me you'd left and given her your flat, but I heard Oreo whine and I knew you'd never abandon him. So, I waited nearby. I can't believe this." She gestured towards Chris and the mess in the kitchen.

Anna rubbed her temple and winced.

"What's happened here?" Sarah asked.

Tom moved over to his unconscious mother, stroking her hair. "Please don't hurt her." Tears spilled from his eyes. "She's my mum. I'll make sure to take her far away. I'll make sure she won't come back here. I'm sorry."

"Why would we—" Sarah scoffed. "She's clearly unhinged, but—"

"What if she hurts *you*, Tom?" Anna said.

"She wouldn't."

"Tom, you're just a child. Look at what she's done to me." Anna held up her wrists where the cable ties had left red marks.

"I can take care of her. I promise." He wiped his runny nose with the back of his hand.

"Tom—"

He choked on a sob and sniffled. "I asked her not to tie you up, but she insisted that you were dangerous. That you were trying to poison her. Is that why you had the rat poison?"

Anna ignored his question. "Tom, you wrote me that note. You said you thought she was dangerous. And your dad…"

"I don't really know what happened to Dad. I don't think she'd hurt anyone without having a reason."

Sarah snorted. "She didn't hesitate to push *me* down the stairs." Apparently satisfied that Tom was no threat she lowered the pistol and offered her hand to Anna to help her up.

Anna took her sister's hand and slowly got to her feet. She frowned. "Chris did what?"

Tom bent over Chris as if trying to shield her. "She knew our food wouldn't last. She was worried—"

"It's okay, Tom. You didn't do anything wrong. It's not your job to protect her." Anna didn't let go of Sarah's hand and instead pulled her sister into a hug. She let Sarah's warmth comfort her and placed her head on her sister's shoulder. "I'm so glad you're here. I thought you were…I was so scared."

"It takes more than the end of the world to get rid of me." Sarah smiled and kissed the top of Anna's head. "Should we…should we tie her up?"

"I'm going to pack a bag," Tom said. "I'm taking her with me as soon as she wakes up."

"Tom—"

"I'll help you in a minute, Tom," Sarah said quickly, smiling at Anna. "I just want to make sure Chris can't attack my sister *again.*"

After binding Chris's hands and ankles, Sarah took the pistol and followed Tom into the spare room.

HALF AN HOUR LATER, Tom sat next to his unconscious mother with her head in his lap. Sarah had made herself and Anna a cup of lukewarm tea. Oreo sat next to Tom with his head placed on Tom's packed bag.

"It's ironic how quickly the tables have turned," Anna said, pressing the warm cup against her temple. The wound stung. She couldn't believe how close she'd come to dying, could still feel the cold knife against her throat, could still see the mad glint in Chris' eyes.

"Why isn't she waking up?" Tom asked.

Sarah shrugged. "I hit her hard. She'll come around." She closed her eyes. "Have you seen what's happening out there, Anna? People are killing each other."

Anna sighed. "I've heard the shooting. Did you walk past Braintree? Things are bad over there."

"I cut through the countryside, but it wasn't much better. It's how I imagined the wild west when we were children."

"I'm not surprised." Anna snorted. "Chris here killed someone ten minutes into the apocalypse."

"It was self-defence." Tom pressed his lips together and scowled. He looked lost sitting on the floor with his legs crossed. He stroked Chris' hair obsessively like a toddler stroking a security blanket.

Anna winced as she thought of the poisoned food. She had to tell him. "It's too late, Tom. She's...your mum is dying." She averted her eyes.

He frowned, confused. "Wh...why?"

"The oatmeal bars I made...I'm sorry."

Sarah gripped her wrist and Anna almost dropped her cup. "What are you saying?" Her eyes widened as fear replaced concern.

Anna's chest tightened. "I—"

"But..." Tom paled as it dawned on him what exactly Anna was saying.

"This isn't your fault, Tom. We won't abandon you, okay? We'll help you find James."

He got up and wrung his hands, his mouth open but no words coming forth. Balling his hands into fists, he kicked over a chair. "How could you?" He stared at Anna with tears in his eyes. "Is that why she isn't waking up?"

Oreo retreated into the kitchen and whimpered. His ears lay flat against the side of his head as he cowered.

"I don't know."

Tom sank to his knees in front of Chris, placing his hands on her thighs. "Mum?" He turned to Anna and sniffled. "Is there anything I can do? Can we make her throw up?"

Anna shook her head. "I think it's too late."

Sarah stammered, closed her mouth, opened it again. "But...but what...what happened?"

"Chris, she..." Anna made a gesture with her hands. "I didn't know what else to do. She's...she's dangerous."

She'd done the right thing. Her sister would understand.

"Why didn't you just ask them to leave?"

"She killed—"

"I get that," Sarah said. "But apparently so have you."

"You're the one holding a pistol." Anna pointed at the weapon in Sarah's hand. She hadn't let go of it since she'd entered the flat. "Where did you find it?"

"I took it off a dead soldier near here," Sarah said.

"And you're prepared to use it." Anna pressed her lips together.

"I suppose so." Sarah fell silent.

Anna watched Tom fussing over his mother. Guilt filled her at the sight. She took a sip of her tea. Another gunshot sounded in the distance. This was the world now. She had done what had to be done.

Chris stirred, her fingers twitching. She lifted her head and moaned. "Tom?"

19

Something was pressed against her cheek. A gentle touch. She leaned into it.

"Mum?"

Chris smiled, comforted by the warmth of Tom's hand.

Anna!

Chris' eyes snapped open. Tom's face faded in and out of focus. "Tom?" Her head pounded. She winced and shifted, squinting. Gradually, the blurred silhouettes surrounding her came back into focus.

"Mum?"

She tried to speak but her tongue lay heavy in her mouth and wouldn't move. Her stomach twisted. The coppery taste of blood mingled with stomach acid. She coughed, the pain at the back of her head excruciating. "Yes?"

Concern filled his eyes. "Are you okay?"

Chris blinked. "Just a mild concuss—" She slurred the word and made another attempt before giving up. "What happened?" Her eyes fell onto Sarah's gun and she was seized with panic. They'd bound her wrists and ankles. She couldn't move.

Focus.

Anna sat next to Sarah with blood-smeared cheeks. The wound on her temple had stopped bleeding. "We don't want to hurt you. You're free to go if you promise to leave without a fight."

Free?

They were letting her go? Something was wrong.

"Can you stand?" Tom asked and when she nodded, he cut her loose and held out both hands, pulling her to her feet. She swayed, holding onto him for support. "We need to leave, Mum."

"I know."

Chris swallowed. She'd ruined everything. She'd tried to keep her family safe. Her husband. Her son. And she'd failed. Both of them.

She looked at Anna and bit her lip. She didn't know what to say.

"It's okay," Anna said. "You were doing it for your son."

Chris forced a smile and nodded. They were letting her go. "May I…may I pack a bag? Take some supplies?"

"I already have," said Tom. "I've prepared enough for us to make it to James'."

James. Tom's best friend. Chris rubbed the back of her head, a bump already noticeable from the blow she had received. James' parents were divorced. His dad owned a farm somewhere near Ware. It wasn't the worst idea.

"And you're just…just letting me go?"

"Mum?" Tom pulled on her sleeve. "I promised that we'd leave peacefully. Please, let's just go."

Chris looked at her son. Pride filled her at the sight. He looked grown up. In charge. And so much like Lester. "Okay."

Tom knelt next to Oreo and wrapped his arms around the dog. He buried his face in Oreo's fur and whispered, "I'll miss you."

Relief washed over Anna as she stood on her balcony, watching Chris and Tom leave. She lingered until they were out of sight and exhaled slowly. Sitting down on the sofa, she rested her head against the wall. "Right. I hope the poison kicks in soon. I don't trust her."

She hadn't thought Chris would give up so easily. She'd expected a fight.

"Yes." Sarah's voice came from the kitchen. A few minutes later she walked into the living room holding a bottle of disinfectant and a packet of cotton wool pads. "I want to clean that wound."

"I'm so glad you're here," Anna said. She scooted to the edge of the sofa and turned her head. She pulled her hair back, exposing her temple. "I thought I'd lost you."

"You know I'm resourceful."

"I thought perhaps you'd gone to find Dad."

Sarah soaked the pad with disinfectant before gingerly dabbing Anna's temple. "Instead of finding you? Never."

"We should…"

"We should check on him. Yes." Sarah continued cleaning Anna's wounds. "Does it hurt?"

Anna shook her head. "Did you check on any of your friends in Colchester?"

"Only my neighbour, Jane." Sarah applied a plaster to Anna's temple. "At first, I was hoping the power would come back on. After a few days, I set out to find you."

"More tea?" Anna asked.

"Yes, please, but I'll make it. You're hurt. I'll feed Oreo too. Poor thing looks thinner than I've ever seen him."

"We need to check how much we have left."

Sarah smiled and kissed Anna's cheek. "I'll make a list."

Sarah disappeared into the kitchen and Oreo followed her.

Anna heard her sister rummaging through the cupboards in the kitchen. "Enough to sit it out for two more weeks." A drawer opened, then closed again.

"I've hidden food in my wardrobe."

"Behind your smelly shoes?"

Anna laughed.

Sarah left the kitchen and Anna heard her opening the bedroom door. "Wow. That's a lot of food."

Anna took a deep breath and relaxed. They'd be fine for a few weeks. Perhaps even a month. They had enough time to come up with a plan. "Do you think Tom will come back once his mum—" Anna couldn't bring herself to say the words.

"I wish he hadn't insisted on leaving with her. We could have helped him."

"I know. I'm scared for him."

"He knows where we are, although—"

Anna frowned. "Although?"

"Aren't you a tiny bit worried he'll come back to…you know…avenge his mum?"

Anna scoffed. "I don't think so. He was afraid of her. Besides, how could I have stopped him? I couldn't poison him as well. He's thirteen and a great kid. You would have liked him. He's intelligent and sweet. It's not his fault Chris is his mother. I mean…look at us and Dad."

Oreo trotted back into the living room and settled down next to Anna.

"I know. I know." A door closed, her sister's voice coming from the spare room, "I've counted fifty bottles of water."

Anna stroked Oreo and crossed her legs, leant back into the cushions and smiled. Sarah was *here*. Unharmed. They'd found each other without having to wander through Essex for years.

They were together.

"What did you say you put the rat poison in?"

"Excuse me?"

"Oatmeal bars or something?"

"Oh. Yes. Chris kept snacking on them."

"I can't find the rest of them. Did she take them with her?"

"I don't know," Anna said. "Perhaps she ate them all." She closed her eyes and exhaled slowly.

No. Anna Greene hadn't been prepared for any kind of emergency, let alone an apocalypse, but considering the odds, she didn't think she'd fared too badly.

They had food and water and a safe place to stay.

"Do you mean these?"

Anna opened her eyes to find Sarah standing in the doorway, an open Tupperware container in her outstretched hand. She nodded.

"It was in the bin, Anna."

Anna frowned. "Maybe Tom threw the rest of them—" Her stomach dropped. She'd cut the slab into six pieces.

There were six pieces left in the Tupperware container.

Sarah pursed her lips. "She didn't trust you either."

Anna knew that, but she hadn't thought Chris wouldn't—

She swallowed, a thousand thoughts swirling around in her mind. Each more terrifying than the previous one. "Oh—" She jumped to her feet, a hand over her stomach. "Sarah! We need to leave."

Sarah put a hand on Anna's shoulder. "Breathe. You're always so quick to panic. I have a gun. We have Oreo. I'm sure we can—"

"What? Barricade the flat? You've met her. She's...she'll try and kill us." Anna pinched the bridge of her nose. She'd tried so hard to make this flat safe for the coming months.

Make it safe for herself and her sister to wait for the worst to pass.

She'd trusted her instincts and given it her best. But the universe wasn't on her side. They needed to pack their bags. Perhaps they could go back to Colchester. Back to Sarah's house.

"Anna?" Sarah grabbed her shoulders and forced Anna to look at her. "It'll be okay. We'll be fine."

Anna exhaled slowly and nodded. Her sister was right. They'd have to find a new place to stay, but at least they were together.

Anna squeezed Sarah's hand and smiled. "We'll figure it out. One day at a time."

THE WEATHER WAS MILD. It wouldn't take them long to get to Ware. A farmhouse would be harder to defend, but it was more likely to have resources. Tom would be happy to see James. He was carrying his laptop under his arm—still convinced he could get some electronics to work with the right equipment. He was still a little boy, but he'd survive.

Chris would make sure of it. She took Tom's hand in hers. His grip tight, he looked at her with red-rimmed eyes.

"What is it?" Chris asked.

"Are you feeling okay?" Tom asked.

"I'm fine. Don't worry about me, sweetie." She flashed him a reassuring smile. Her head still pounded, but she'd feel better in a few days.

She'd ruined things with Anna, but they'd find somewhere else to stay. She was a nurse. A valuable addition to any group of survivors. She was confident they'd find a new shelter. A new place where nobody knew of her past. Of Mike and Lester. Or of what had just happened with the Greene sisters.

Chris would try hard to fit in and keep Tom safe.

They'd move on, but Chris would never forget Anna's *kindness*. She'd never forget the small flat on Fifth Avenue, and perhaps one day, they'd meet again…

End

NOTE FROM THE AUTHOR

Thank you for reading. I hope you enjoyed it.

If you'd like to check out more of my work, have a look at my first completed series, The End We Saw. I've recently released an omnibus consisting of all five novellas available exclusively on Amazon.

If you like your apocalypse with supernatural powers, and your characters driven by guilt and redemption, you'll enjoy this fast-paced series set in London.

If you liked "Darkness Within," please consider leaving a review either on Amazon or Goodreads.

Don't want to miss out on new books? Sign up to my mailing list over at lspencerauthor.com and be the first to receive news, updates and pictures of my dog.

You'll receive a free short story for signing up, and I hope to share more stories with my subscribers soon. Your email address will never be shared and you're free to unsubscribe at any time. No hard feelings; I promise.

Thank you again.

Printed in Great Britain
by Amazon